ROY LEWIS

A Kind of Transaction

An Eric Ward novel

THE CRIME CLUB
An Imprint of HarperCollins *Publishers*

First published in Great Britain in 1991
by The Crime Club, an imprint of
HarperCollins Publishers, 77–85 Fulham Palace Road,
Hammersmith, London W6 8JB

9 8 7 6 5 4 3 2 1

A catalogue record for this book is
available from the British Library

ISBN 0 00 232364 8

Photoset in Linotron Baskerville by
Rowland Phototypesetting Ltd
Bury St Edmunds, Suffolk
Printed and bound in Great Britain by
HarperCollins Book Manufacturing, Glasgow

Commerce: A kind of transaction in which A plunders from B the goods of C and for compensation B picks the pocket of D of money belonging to E.

Ambrose Bierce: *The Devil's Dictionary*

CHAPTER 1

1

The walls of the villa were painted white, glaringly bright under the hot, late afternoon sun. The pool was a bright blue, shimmering in the heat, and the sun-loungers on the patio were orange and green and red, the sun-umbrella yellow, shading the white wrought-iron table on which an empty bottle and some glasses stood. From the vantage-point under the pine trees of the craggy hillside the house and the patio and the pool presented a harsh splash of foreign colour against the deep blue of the sea and the lavender green of the scrub that encircled the house.

As he crouched uncomfortably among the bushes on the hill, Soldier could smell crushed rosemary and there was a faint odour of pine in his nostrils, but he was barely aware of either. Through powerful field glasses he scanned the villa, slowly, carefully, methodically. The dirt track that wound its painful way down the crag was dusty and rock-strewn. It was partly shaded by mean, spindly pines but as it neared the high, white-painted wall that encircled the house, it opened out, a dangerous no man's land for strangers, a wide swathe of cleared, levelled bush where a car might park or a man might die.

The walls around the house were eight feet high. The ditch beneath added another two feet, making the wall difficult to scale, but the field glasses picked up a weak point: a craggy promontory that was elevated above the west wall, a leaning tree, a long, dangerous, but not impossible drop. From there it was twenty feet to thick undergrowth, spiky fan palms, limestone crag and trees, before the low wall surrounding the swimming pool in front of the house was reached, across a brief, startlingly green stretch of lawn.

A slow drop of sweat crawled down Soldier's nose. He flicked it away with an irritated finger. He needed a swim. But not before he was sure. Carefully, the field glasses traversed the house itself: the locked doors, the *rejas* barring the windows, black against the shining white of the walls, the castellated turret with the higher terrace, the long, long drop beyond the far wall with its cowled sun-shelter to the pounding surf two hundred feet below.

Down there the rocks would rip a man and bury him, leaving nothing but scraps for the fish.

He did one last sweep of the house. There was one thing he was pleased about, at least. There were no dogs.

Grunting, he rose to his feet, muscles aching at holding the crouching position for so long. He looked out to sea: two small boats, white-sailed against the sharp blue and then the distant haze—the haze he'd fade into once the job was done. He packed away the field glasses and reached for his shirt. The muscles rippled in his chest: he admired them for a moment, the two-week tan enhancing them, making them gleam under the light sheen of sweat. He'd swum every day, and after dark he'd pounded the hill road, timing it and keeping fit at the same time. He'd be having—and needing—one chance only. He could go down now, for he knew the movements of the inhabitants of the villa. That was a mistake they made: regularity. A man who didn't change his ways could take his last breath without even knowing it.

The thought made him smile grimly. He pulled the short-sleeved shirt over his head and let it hang outside his shorts. His trainers were scuffed and dirty from climbing the rough crags and jogging along the dusty roads but after today he'd be wearing more elegant shoes. The money—the other half of the contract—would be waiting for him in Madrid. He moved slowly through the trees, ducking below the branches of the pines, skirting the sharp spines of the undergrowth and scrambling over the rough ground until he reached the top of the hill.

He emerged from the trees to the rough track. The car was a mile and a half away. He checked his watch and began to run, a steady jogging that hardly raised his heartbeat, but one that would bring him to the car in a measured time. Dust pounded up under his feet and cicadas whirred ahead of him, falling silent as he passed. High above his head a lone eagle soared, wheeling, silent, drifting on the thermals.

The car—a small hired Fiat—was parked inconspicuously at the edge of the track. He had deliberately chosen a typical tourist hire car—cheap, numerous on the coast, and paid for with a stolen credit card. He saw no reason to spend more than he had to in this rat hole of a place . . . and besides, his presence would be more difficult to trace if he used stolen credit cards to pay his way. He smiled again: it was a weakness, he knew, lifting cards that way, but it gave him pleasure.

The rest was business.

He unlocked the car and drove down to the town, five miles distant.

There was little there. A large enough town for the area, it boasted twenty or more restaurants and cafés, a couple of discos, and a long, curving beach. It was a resort used by the Spanish themselves, so it had not been cluttered by high rise developments, though a number of villas had now been built on the outskirts by foreigners—Dutch, Swiss, German, and a few English. Among them would be more than a few villains, Soldier guessed, salting away earnings where the British taxman would find it difficult to trace. But it wasn't his scene: he came from a rawer, colder part of the world. Sun and swimming was fine for a while, but he preferred his own haunts, and a language he understood.

Not that language was a problem. Money was all that was necessary. It was all he needed with the whore.

He took a swim in the late afternoon, a light meal at the restaurant on the beach and then a slow cigar as the sun gleamed on the horizon. Then it was time to get rid of the ache in his loins, the ache that always came before he had a contract to complete. It was like a cleansing, an emptying of all thought other than the one.

She had broad hips, dark thighs as she sprawled in the odorous room above the café. Her skin was greasy, her armpits damp as he entered her, grunting, vicious and urgent. He heard the intake of breath as he hurt her and it stimulated him: he grasped her hair with his right hand and dragged it sideways, half off the bed. He clamped his left hand over her mouth as he hammered at her, the hard muscles of his stomach knotting, his powerful thighs rigid as she writhed under him. Then the explosion came and was gone, and he rolled away, as dissatisfied as ever as he listened to the harsh, panting, hurt animal sounds she made in the darkness. He said nothing. He washed quickly in the handbasin in the corner of the room, dressed, threw her some money and left.

He felt light, and clean and deadly.

At the rented apartment he changed into black slacks and shirt, with dark blue trainers. He locked the apartment door behind him, carried the pistol in the small black bag strapped to his belt. The Fiat took him quickly away from the town. He checked his watch: it was nine o'clock. The villa would be empty, though security lights would have been left burning. Creatures of habit, the owners would not return until eleven at the earliest. He parked the car in the usual place and began to jog down the track. The moon was high, a crescent that silvered the trees and made the track ahead of him gleam whitely. He was still breathing steadily when he reached the top of the hill and entered the trees.

It was easy enough crossing the hill in moonlight. Within minutes he could hear the pounding of the surf and then he was out on the crag, with the villa gleaming below him.

He moved on down through the trees, cursing softly as spines caught at his shirt, until he reached the promontory above the villa wall. He grasped the branch of the leaning pine tree and looked down. Moonlight distorted the scene but he had watched and measured in his mind's eye and he was confident. He grabbed at the trunk, eased himself along the swaying branch, hand over hand, and then dropped, without thinking. He landed on his feet, crashing into the undergrowth and there was blood on his face as he was scored by sharp, needle-like bushes. He paid no attention to it. He hurried through the bushes, across the lawn and under the lights of the patio to the back of the villa. He reached up to the *rejas* on the lower window and hauled himself upwards, over the top of the protecting bars on to the sloping roof of the kitchen. Lightly he moved across the tiles until he reached the coping of the terrace below the castellated bedroom. He pulled himself up, heaving his upper body across the low wall, and dropped to the broad terrace beyond.

The door presented no problems. The *rejas* that should have protected it could not resist his brute strength. The black-painted wrought-iron work was cemented into the wall but was a deterrent rather than protection. He placed his feet against the wall, gripped the *rejas* and threw his whole weight backwards. The ironwork squealed, bent, then gave way slowly. He pulled the *rejas* out with a sudden surge. He kicked in the door easily enough: the sound of cracking timber did not bother him for there was no one to listen. The light above the terrace would possibly reveal the damage, however; he smashed it with the gun butt. Then he entered the bedroom with the gun in his right hand, a small torch in his left. The room was lavishly furnished, but he paid no attention. He moved to the other three rooms: they were all empty, as he had known they would be. Downstairs, there was a single light burning in the hallway, but he could dispense with the torch and there was enough illumination to discover the drinks cabinet.

Soldier poured himself a glass of beer and tasted it. He wrinkled his nose in disgust, then sat down, looking around him, sipping the beer with no great enjoyment. Spanish beer was not a patch on Newcastle Brown. He glanced at his watch. They would be home about eleven. In the hallway a clock chimed, confirming his watch. It was nine-thirty. Time to get to work.

He began in the sitting-room, methodically, testing each drawer, checking for the documents. Then he worked through the rest of the house, downstairs and upstairs. It took him twenty minutes to find the safe. There was no point in trying to crack it. He didn't have the skills anyway. He'd just have to wait.

He was used to waiting.

Prison did that for a man. The porridge he had done at Durham had been easy. The screws knew his reputation and left him alone; and he didn't give them reason to get rough. He wanted out—he enjoyed life outside. So he did his porridge and kept his mouth shut. You could sit, and wait it out.

The problem was the ache. It wasn't all that bad for him in prison, because there was no action waiting. But outside . . . he thought of the whore and his body stirred again. When he had a contract to complete, there was always the ache. It had to be assuaged before he could become the cool, controlled soldier that he'd built his reputation on, the mechanic who did a clean job, made no mistakes. But the ache—it never changed: before action, it was always there.

He checked his watch. Ten-fifteen. It wouldn't be long now.

Even as he thought it he heard a car on the hill. He hefted the gun in his hand, muzzle raised to the ceiling, and moved to the window, screened by the curtain. Lights slashed across the hillside, lifting and falling along the track and Soldier frowned. They were early. But it made no difference to him. He watched as the car came down the hill and crossed the open space.

The lights were not killed, as he expected, and the engine was still running. Soldier frowned, grunting softly to himself.

There was a short interval, and then the slamming of a car door. Soldier peered past the curtain, parting it slightly with the gun muzzle. He realized the car was turning, going back up the hill as the wall door to the villa was unlocked and opened.

He moved away from the window, edgy. Things weren't going according to plan. They shouldn't have come back until eleven: they followed a pattern, eating out, returning about the same time each evening. He stepped towards the hallway, hidden by the wall, and he heard steps on the patio, the front door opening, slamming, steps in the hall. There was a muffled curse, something thrown violently to the floor. It skidded across the marbled hallway into his line of vision.

It was a handbag.

Soldier stepped out into the hallway. It was the woman. She stared at him, shocked, saw the gun and her mouth opened to scream but no sound came. She stood there, gaping in terror, rigid, and then as she backed away against the wall Soldier stepped forward, grabbed her by the front of her low-necked dress and pressed the gun against her temple.

She moaned in panic and her knees began to buckle. He pressed her against the door, his thighs hard against hers, half holding her up, as her blue eyes rolled wildly.

'Where is he?' Soldier asked gratingly.

It took her several seconds to reply. He tightened the grip on her dress, twisting his fingers viciously and the material began to tear. She licked lips dry with fear. 'He . . . he's still at the restaurant.'

'Why?'

'We quarrelled . . . we had a fight.'

'You took a cab back?'

She nodded quickly, and her lipstick was blotched as she rubbed her hand against her mouth. 'What . . . what do you want?'

'But he'll be back?'

Her eyes were wide with panic but it was not all for herself. 'I don't know.'

She knew.

So did Soldier. The man had nowhere else to go. He stared at the woman, thinking, and then he turned, dragged her across the hallway and threw her into the sitting-room. She staggered against the settee, and fell to the thick rug. Soldier raised his gun. She stared at him, her mouth open and gasping as she lay spreadeagled on the floor. She began to moan.

Soldier levelled the gun.

Her dress was torn at the throat and her skin was tanned, even on the swell of her half-exposed breast. Sprawled as she was, her dress had ridden up over her long, slim legs and he stared at her, his eyes dwelling on the soft curve of her thighs.

She was different from the whore: she had class, she smelled different, in spite of the fear, and her flesh was not so heavy. She was different: long, dark hair, blue eyes, a slim figure but high breasted, a woman to die for, perhaps.

But not him . . . His finger began to squeeze the trigger gently.

'Please . . .' she moaned.

Cordite.

If he shot her now, when the target finally arrived he might smell the cordite, run . . . Why make life difficult? Soldier lowered the gun.

He smiled, and sat down. He looked at the woman's exposed thighs, and the whore on the beach was forgotten as the ache in his loins was back. There would be time . . . he'd hear the car anyway, as it came over the hill.

Negligently he waved the gun at her.

'You don't cook for him,' he said.

Sprawled on the floor, shocked, she made no reply.

'You don't cook. You and him, you go out every night. To the restaurant.'

She didn't know what was moving in his mind, slow, turgid, but exciting. She nodded, staring at him as though she were hypnotized.

'If you don't cook for him, you must have other talents.'

Her lack of comprehension was tinged with alarm. She moved carefully, rising on her elbow. 'Please, I don't know what you want—'

He did.

'Get up.'

She stared at him, her mouth still sagging in panic, but then she struggled to rise, eager to do his bidding in the relief she felt that the gun was no longer menacing her. Soldier grinned. He waved the gun at her, describing a lazy, menacing arc with the muzzle.

'Now take off your dress.'

'What?'

'You heard me.'

'But I—'

'I won't say it again.'

She understood. Her eyes widened, and her left hand tugged at the tear in her dress. 'No, please—'

He stood up. It would have been too easy if she had been acquiescent, less pleasurable. He preferred it this way, in any case.

He stepped towards her and she began to back away; he moved more swiftly and as she opened her mouth to scream he hit her with his left hand, a short arm jab to the cheekbone. He felt the flesh open as she went down. In the dim light he saw the red weal on her face, and the first trickle of dark blood. He leaned over her and tore away the lower part of her dress. She moaned, half-conscious.

'No . . . don't . . .'

She was rigid with fear as he stood over her, legs braced

apart, the gun still in his right hand. He stared down at her, enjoying the moment, feeling the desire rise and rage in his groin.

Her legs were long and lean and tanned. She wore lacy briefs; he leaned over her and pressed the muzzle of the gun against her stomach, slipped it inside her briefs and with a quick jerk tore them away.

Soldier giggled, a high-pitched, excited sound. In the dim light he saw the weal along the inside of her thigh, where the muzzle of the gun had scored the skin. She was rigid with fear now, watching him with terrified eyes. He waved the muzzle in front of her face, traced its cold mouth down the length of her body, touched it delicately against the soft inside of her thighs and he heard her breath grow ragged, rasping with terror. Her fear increased his desire.

Soldier put down his gun.

2

The moors above Slocum House were famous for their grouse. Sir Henry Slocum controlled them well through his keepers, and had been known, occasionally, to allow some of his parliamentarian friends and colleagues to use them for weekend sport. That would have been when he wanted some political favours from them, or needed them to support his point of view in some debate in which he had an interest. For most of the time he used the moors to entertain his business acquaintances: there was no possibility of buying time on his moors as many Japanese businessmen did on some of the other local estates. They came in from Heathrow to Newcastle, and cars were laid on for them at the airport to whisk them down to the Durham moors to try their hands at the grouse. But not on the Slocum estates . . . not unless they came on Slocum business.

There had been a party out on the Slocum estate that afternoon. Eric Ward had not been one of them. When Anne had told him they had been invited he had suggested they politely decline: he did not care for the right-wing Tory owner of Slocum House. Anne had insisted that even if they did not appear on the moors, they should certainly turn up for dinner in the evening.

'We can plead other business in the morning and afternoon,' she argued, 'but Sir Henry's more than hinted that meeting some of his other guests could be advantageous.'

'In what way?'

'For Morcomb Estates,' Anne replied testily. 'What else?'

Eric stretched his long legs out easily in front of him and squinted up at his wife in the late afternoon sunshine. The light brought reddish tints out in her hair as she leaned against the terrace wall with the green slope of the hills rising behind her. He recalled the first time he had seen her, riding in the hills above Sedleigh Hall, young, slim . . . She was more mature now but could still make his heart lift. She was a beautiful woman, and in some things he indulged her. 'Who else is going to be there?'

'Slocum hasn't provided me with a guest list, but I gather there's going to be quite a few.'

Eric groaned. 'Not one of those high table, below the salt affairs, where all the women will be checking whether their husbands have been slighted by the placing they've been given!'

'*Your* wife won't be checking.'

'Because you're not seen as an appendage of mine. You're a businesswoman, major shareholder and managing director of Morcomb Estates Ltd, not a sweet stay-at-home wife.'

'Is that what you would want me to be?'

'Hey! I've got what I want. I'm just moaning about *me* doing the wifely bit really, since I'm the appendage on evenings like Slocum's. It's I who'll be doing the checking, to be certain you're above the salt.'

'So you'll come?'

'Could you doubt it, darling?'

She eyed him suspiciously. 'And you'll behave yourself?'

Eric pulled a face. 'Won't you allow me just one little checking?'

She grimaced in return. 'I don't think you need worry about the seating arrangements. I'm sure Sir Henry won't slight me. I think he's got a soft spot for me.'

'He goes for your soft spots whenever he can, certainly,' Eric said, and grinned.

'I know how to deal with gropers.'

'Why are you looking at me like that?'

The invitations had been sent out to at least forty people, and it seemed that most, if not all had turned up. The dining-hall in Slocum House was full; the age-darkened oak table had been laid with glittering silverware and the chandelier threw sparkling shafts of light on the dresses of the women, who had turned out in all their finery. The men wore dinner jackets, with the exception of Sir Henry himself, who presided in tails. He was a tall, well-built man, an ex-Guards officer who had seen service in the Western Desert in the Second World War. He had taken a safe Conservative seat in the Midlands some thirty years ago. He had announced he would not be standing at the next election, but there was nothing doddery about him: his full, white moustache bristled as fiercely as ever, his apple cheeks were bright and there was the usual mischievous light in his small blue eyes. There was much of the schoolboy about him still, and he certainly did find Anne attractive. He had made that obvious over pre-dinner drinks, one hand on her bare shoulder, leaning confidingly to talk to her while Eric watched at a distance. Perhaps that was why Eric disliked him; but Eric didn't care for his jingoistic brand of politics either, and some of his business practices had left a bad taste in northern mouths of recent years, when he had closed down several subsidiaries on Tyneside.

Eric was separated from Anne at dinner, of course: he found himself next to a flirtatious young woman called Caroline who was enchanted by the young man on her left, so he was spared the necessity of indulging in small talk with her. On his right sat Barry Wincanton of Northern Oil. Having partaken freely of the gin before dinner, he seemed determined to top off the exercise by drinking as much of Slocum's wine as possible and there was little room for conversation there. Eric was pleased. He was happy to sit, make the occasional comment, and observe.

Perhaps twenty of the other guests were well known to Eric, businessmen, a couple of doctors, the obligatory clergyman who could be relied upon to tell religious jokes.

Charles Davison was also there. He caught Eric's glance early on and nodded coolly. Eric gave him a wintry smile in return. They had not met since the Paulson business, though Davison still held a retainer from Morcomb Estates. Anne knew Eric disliked Davison, but an inherent stubbornness made her use Davison still; Eric was disinclined to tell her the main reason for his dislike, for in such a recounting he would not himself appear in too bright a light. In Eric's view, Davison was untrustworthy; he sailed too close to the wind on occasions, his view of business ethics was a clouded one and he was a bit too sharp in his practices, for Eric's liking. The one occasion they had crossed swords still rankled in Eric's mind.

'Bloody Chinese,' Wincanton muttered.

'Sorry?'

'Bloody Chinese. That guy over there. Them and the Japanese, they're taking over the world. Let 'em stay in Hong Kong, say I.'

He took a long draught of red wine. Eric looked at him coolly. Wincanton was about forty years of age, heavily built and inclining to corpulence. His red-veined eyes were bleary and resentful. Eric glanced across the table to the man Wincanton was complaining about. He was a small, neat, dark man of indeterminate age, his greying hair carefully parted, a seemingly perpetual smile on his chubby lips, a moon face that might on occasion disarm colleagues. 'Does he have business over here?'

'That's the bloody trouble. He's been invited here this evening because of proposals he's put up to old Slocum regarding Teesside. A rejuvenation of shipping interests—a Cleveland consortium. Slocum's over the moon about it, of course: if he can pull some Government chestnuts out of the fire here in the North-East by pushing through a deal with the bloody Chinese, he might end up with another gong when he retires at the next election.' Wincanton grimaced unpleasantly and glared along the table towards Slocum. 'All I'll get out of it is the odd glass of wine. Slocum's seen Northern Oil's proposals, yet he puts me all the way down here, well away from that bloody Chink up there.'

Way down here, beside Eric Ward. Eric smiled to himself. So that was why Wincanton was attacking the bottle so vigorously. Slocum was showing him, by the seat placing, that he stood no chance against the Chinese bid. He glanced across to Anne, seated near the object of Wincanton's ire. She caught his quiet smile, and returned it, warmly, but questioningly. He could tell her later that it wasn't only the women who worried about seat placings.

As for the Chinese businessman, he seemed all affability as he carried on an animated conversation with the women seated either side of him, courteous in his measured attention to each, smiling, making them laugh, charming in his little asides. They clearly enjoyed his company, and Eric watched him for a while, amused at the practised ease with which he held their attention. Sir Henry Slocum himself, at the head of the table was watching the man also, a fixed smile on his face, but now he was rising to his feet.

'Well, ladies and gentlemen, I think it's appropriate if I say a few words of welcome to you all, before we move out to the withdrawing-room where coffee will be served. Always did hate havin' it at the dinner table. It's good to see so many old friends . . .' Eric felt Slocum's glance slip past him as he waved his welcoming glass to take in the general gathering around the table. 'But it'd be remiss of me if I didn't extend a special welcome to Simon Chan.

After all, he's come a long way to be with us here tonight, and has uttered not a single word of complaint when faced with our culinary offerings here at Slocum House, which are of course, far inferior to his own South-East Asian delicacies.'

The Chinese businessman smiled, but his eyes were expressionless as he bowed slightly, where he sat.

'I am delighted to see Simon here for reasons other than social; I am pleased to say he has exciting plans for the development of his company's interests here in the North-East, and there are many of us in the Government who are delighted that a company of such eminence should be looking to this area for investment. Mr Chan, if I may be so formal, you are very welcome, and we look forward to a swift determination of the outstanding issues . . .'

'Not if *we* can bloody well help it,' Barry Wincanton muttered through clenched teeth.

The party began to break up about eleven. Anne and Eric had decided to stay at the flat in Newcastle rather than make the long drive back to Sedgefield Hall; since his wife had been in animated conversation with the Chinese businessman for the last twenty minutes Eric had made no attempt to suggest they leave, even though some of the Teesside contingent had already gone. Coffee was still being served to those who wanted it, and Eric had availed himself of the offer of a brandy. He could manage one without trouble: he'd taken little wine over dinner, and of late he'd had little trouble with his eyes: the glaucoma appeared to have been arrested.

'So, Eric, it's going to be a late night, hey?'

Eric turned and smiled coolly at Charles Davison. He had managed to avoid him most of the evening, but it would be churlish to cut him now. He shrugged. 'When my wife's talking business, I don't like to curtail her.'

Davison grinned. It softened the craggy lines of his handsome features; he was a tall, well-built man with eyelashes that a woman would envy and a dress sense that served him well. He was well known on the northern cocktail circuit; having married a wealthy woman older than himself, he had quickly established an important legal practice in Newcastle, of a kind rather more elevated than Eric's—he dealt with only the best clients. Like Morcomb Estates. He was still in his forties, fit, tanned, and confident. 'Looks like she's cultivating Chan to effect. Morcomb Estates are doing well,' he said. 'How about your own practice on the Quayside?'

'It turns over an honest penny.'

'Unlike some you could mention, hey?' There was a challenge in Davison's brown eyes which belied the lightness of his tone. He had not forgotten the deal he and Eric had struck over Paulson,* though it was something Eric preferred to forget.

'Horses for courses, Davison. I do what suits me. If you want to ride wilder stallions, that's up to you.'

'Ever the cautious one, Eric.' Davison laughed gently. 'You're a fool. Petty criminals, the odd shipping contract . . . that's not the way to a successful practice. But then, why should I tell you that? I'm sure others say the same . . .'

His eyes dwelled on Anne, making her way across to them with the Chinese businessman in tow. Eric felt cold momentarily at the thought that Anne might have been discussing him with the man she had retained as corporate lawyer to Morcomb Estates, but then he realized Davison was simply out to needle him. He stayed quiet as Anne came near and introduced Simon Chan to Davison before turning to Eric.

'And this is my husband.'

'Mr Chan.'

'I am delighted to make your acquaintance.' The man's English was impeccable, the accent slight. His handshake

* *A Necessary Dealing.*

was firm, his eyes friendly. 'Your wife has told me a little about you, and there have been others . . . Perhaps you would receive my card? Chinese names, I know, often cause difficulties with Westerners, who are not certain which name to use. It's why I, like so many of my fellow businessmen, have adopted a Western name—in my case, Simon. It makes life easier.' He handed Eric a business card in the Asian fashion, holding it delicately between the first finger and thumb of each hand, making a polite presentation of it. Eric glanced at the card.

'Malaysia Mobile Berhad . . . I was told you were from Hong Kong.'

'You were misinformed,' Simon Chan said, exposing gold-capped teeth as he smiled almost apologetically. 'I suppose it is a natural reaction when one meets a Chinese businessman in England to presume he comes from Hong Kong. My company is based in Kuala Lumpur, though we have interests in Hong Kong. I myself am Singaporean in origin. It can be a confusing world, can it not, if information received is not correct?'

'Too confusing for me, Mr Chan,' Davison said easily. 'I hope you don't mind me taking my leave, but I've a heavy day tomorrow. I'll see you in the afternoon, Anne?'

She nodded. Simon Chan was watching Eric. It was unlikely he would be able to sense the dislike that lay between the two solicitors, but Eric felt, nevertheless, that his feelings were being laid bare by the scrutiny.

After Davison had left them to say good night to Sir Henry, Chan beamed upon Eric. 'I have been having a most stimulating conversation with your wife, who has been telling me about the progress of her company. I am much impressed by what she has achieved with Morcomb Estates. In such a short time. In Kuala Lumpur Chinese women—if not the Malays—make good businesswomen. I now understand the English can similarly show skills where mere men in their ignorant way might expect none.'

'Mr Chan's been throwing compliments around all evening, Eric,' Anne said, smiling.

'Not mere compliments. Truth. The fact is, Mrs Ward, I am impressed. I would like to converse about possibilities further. You see, Mr Ward, my company in Kuala Lumpur is looking for diversification opportunities. The Japanese have shown the way with major investment in the car industry in the North-East . . . indeed, they have virtually taken over the car industry in Malaysia too. But we must learn by example. For Malaysia, there are traditional links, of course, with Britain, but of recent years as overseas investment in Malaysia has proliferated, so we feel now it is time we expanded beyond our Asian shipping, timber and construction activities into the European market.'

'I was explaining to Mr Chan that Morcomb Estates are also looking for diversification opportunities, that we had recently taken over a construction company and were entering the field of distribution in our Wallsend operation.'

Simon Chan nodded. 'This I find most interesting.' He glanced around him appreciatively. 'Occasions such as this, at Sir Henry's home, are not common practice in Malaysia, where business tends to be done in the club, or a restaurant, or in the office environment. But I find it . . . conducive. One can relax, and also learn. I feel, if I may say so, there is business Mrs Ward and I can do. I shall be arranging a further meeting for later in the week at Morcomb Estates' headquarters. I believe there are enterprises we can further together.'

'You're committed to the Teesside activity?' Eric asked.

Simon Chan smiled enigmatically. 'Sir Henry would have me *believe* so.'

'He can be a persuasive man.'

'He is a politician. They often hear only their own arguments, not the comments of others.' He paused. 'But enough of business talk.' He turned to Anne. 'You must tell of your lovely home. I understand it is most beautiful . . .'

Eric finished his brandy. He glanced around. Davison

had left, and the numbers in the room were thinning out. Sir Henry Slocum was heading in their direction. His eyes were fixed on Anne. His voice boomed out as he advanced, a battleship ploughing through the crowd.

'Now then, my dear, don't get too carried away by oriental charm. Remember you've old friends to look after—like your host! Not drinking, Eric? No?' He turned to Chan. 'Your glass is empty, Simon. Don't tell me you won't have another brandy. It's the Chinese tipple, isn't that so?'

'Not when there is the danger of business being mixed with pleasure, Sir Henry.'

'Well, you won't do much business with Eric,' Slocum announced, and guffawed. He grabbed Anne's elbow, drawing her away. 'You can try, though many of us have failed. But try by all means. You'll excuse us, won't you, gentlemen?'

He laughed, dragged a reluctant Anne away towards the group near the fireplace and Simon Chan observed Eric quietly for a few seconds. 'As you say, Mr Ward, a persuasive man. He appears fond of your wife.'

'They've known each other for some years. Sir Henry knew Anne's father.'

'Ah yes . . .' Chan watched Eric carefully for a few moments. 'I am told by your wife that you are a lawyer.'

'That's right.'

'In Malaysia, legal skills are much prized, and lawyers play an important part in business.'

Eric shrugged, suddenly defensive. 'I have some business interests.'

'But not in conjunction with your wife.'

'Marriage and business can sometimes make bad bedfellows.'

'You are wise. Morcomb Estates is, of course, part of your wife's inheritance, I understand. But your other business . . . ?'

Eric shrugged. 'I'm on the board of the merchant

bankers, Martin and Channing, in London. But that's part-time, and even there, in a sense, I'm representing Anne's interest. But I have my own legal practice, on the Quayside, in Newcastle.'

Simon Chan nodded. His eyes were hooded. 'This practice . . . in what do you specialize?'

Eric laughed. The thought of using the word 'specialize' in relation to his practice was amusing. The Quayside was the right location for him: it kept him in touch with Newcastle and the north, reminded him of his roots, kept his feet on the ground, made him face realities other than the broad sweep of the Morcomb Estates and the easy life he could lead in the Northumberland hills . . . the kind of life he sometimes thought Anne wanted him to live. But he needed his independence . . . and he owed his Quayside practice to no one.

'You do not specialize?' Simon Chan asked, puzzled.

'Hardly. No, I deal with whoever comes in through the door. We've built up a certain marine practice, insurance, shipping, charterparty work, that sort of thing, not least because we're based on Tyneside and have easy access to Teesside. And we do a fair amount of criminal defence work—but there's no money in that! No, it's a small practice, but it deals with people . . . and maybe that's what I want.'

'There are other lawyers, like Mr Davison . . .'

'That's right,' Eric said shortly. 'There are other lawyers.'

There was a short silence. Simon Chan's eyes seemed to bore into Eric. Softly the man said, 'The comment was made this evening . . . your name came up . . . you were once a policeman, is that not so?'

'That's right. But it seems a long time ago, now.'

'And you moved from the police force to start a legal practice? This is not very usual, I think.'

'I took a part-time degree while I was in the police, and became a solicitor once I left.' Eric hesitated. There seemed no reason to tell Chan why he left, or to explain about his constant struggle with glaucoma.

'So you have a small practice, and you deal with criminal matters. There would have been much crime to handle as a policeman. I presume that as a result of your previous existence in the police you still have contacts with those who are of—shall we say—the underworld?'

Eric laughed. 'Not exactly. Of course, while I was in the police I got to know a lot of people, villains included, and I made use of the network.'

'Informers, you mean?'

Eric shrugged. 'I prefer the word contacts.'

Simon Chan's eyes were lidded; he looked down at his hands. They were smooth, and pudgy and careful. 'I understand. Do you ever, in your practice, have occasion to undertake work in regard to . . . missing persons?'

'Occasionally. As I suggested, we have a sort of general practice.'

'Small firms can be discreet, can they not?'

Eric stared at him. 'Lawyers are all accustomed to treating their clients' confidences as sacrosanct, as far as the law allows.'

'And you believe in the law?'

'I wouldn't be a lawyer, otherwise.' Eric laughed. 'In spite of the barbs that are thrown at the profession. You know—when they say "You can trust me, I'm a lawyer," they mean it as a joke.'

'Yes.' Simon Chan smiled. 'I am accustomed to Western humour.' He was silent for a little while. 'Discretion,' he went on, 'is very important to a businessman. Delicacy of touch is a virtue, sensitivity a necessary quality. And there are occasions when certain matters must be handled in such a way that . . . I wonder, Mr Ward, if I could be frank with you?'

Eric smiled. 'If you mean you want to have a private conversation with me which shall remain private, please feel free. You're not my client, but I can remain discreet outside office hours.'

Simon Chan smiled. 'I don't doubt it. As for my being a client of yours, this is what I have in mind . . . I wonder whether you would be interested in undertaking an assignment on behalf of Malaysia Mobile Berhad?'

Eric hesitated. 'It depends on whether it's something I think I could handle. You mean you have a legal problem here in England?'

'Let's just say I have a problem . . . and I think you might be able to help me. If you are interested, perhaps we could discuss it.' Chan glanced around the room casually. 'I think this occasion is . . . not suitable. And I leave for Kuala Lumpur on Friday. I shall be at Morcomb Estates' premises for a business discussion on Thursday afternoon. Perhaps you and I could have dinner Thursday evening?'

'For me, that presents no problem,' Eric replied.

'So what exactly does he want?' Anne asked as they got into bed at the Newcastle flat.

'I've no idea. And since he wants me to be discreet, I wouldn't tell you anyway.'

Anne plumped up her pillow and sniffed. 'There are no secrets between husband and wife.'

'Quite. So what deal does he hope to strike with you?'

Anne snuggled beneath the covers and reached for him, curling her arm around his waist. 'Not sure, yet. He's a bit vague. But I got the impression he wants to look at our plans for the distribution network at Wallsend. He's attracted, I think, by the potential it offers for entry across the North Sea to the Scandinavian markets.'

'He's not even into the North-East yet!'

'Confucius, he say, Chinese man who not look forward fall flat on face.'

'I get the impression Mr Simon Chan rarely falls flat on his face,' Eric demurred. 'He's the kind of man who never gives too much away. But you think he'll work with Morcomb Estates?'

'I think it's on the cards. It could be an important contract,' Anne murmured. 'It would give us a great start at Wallsend, and there's no real reason why it should be contingent upon Slocum's Teesside deal.'

'And Sir Henry, no doubt, would welcome any investment in the North-East—and claim it as a triumph of his own.'

Anne snorted into the pillow. 'Sir Henry is an old fool.'

'Goat.'

'As I recall, you're Capricorn yourself.'

Eric turned to her, slipping his arm around her neck and drawing her close. 'Only in inclination, my love, only in inclination.'

Sir Henry Slocum had been right about one thing, at least: the Chinese enjoyed brandy, if Simon Chan was anything to go by. Eric had joined him in a private room in his Gateshead hotel and Chan had immediately poured him a large glass of cognac. They were alone, and it was clear that the conversation was to be private—Eric had been introduced to several polite, smooth-featured young men of Chan's entourage, but none of them was invited to join them for dinner. Chan had ordered a Cantonese banquet, and the hotel had managed to come up to scratch—sufficiently so for Chan to indulge in pleasantries only, while he discreetly assisted Eric in his chopstick manipulation of the food. Wine was served with the meal, but Chan stayed with the brandy. Eric barely touched his wine.

'Do you know very much about business in Malaysia, Eric?' Simon Chan asked at last.

'I'm afraid not.'

Chan waved his brandy glass thoughtfully. 'The country has a problem of an ethnic nature. Those who would regard themselves as indigenous—the Malays, or the *bumiputera* as they call themselves—are actually in the minority in terms of population. There is a strong Indian contingent—very much retail and small business-based, as you might imagine. And then there are the Chinese. Many of them were, of course, born in Malaysia, but . . . they are Chinese. It is the Chinese who really run big business in Malaysia—but it is the Malays who wield political power under the constitution.'

'That leads to problems?'

'Of a kind. There is a certain discrimination against the Chinese Malaysians. Education . . . housing . . . preferences are given to the indigenous Malays. It is perhaps of little consequence in educational terms. We Chinese still do the business; we fund our own schools outside the state system, our own universities . . .' He drained his glass and poured himself another brandy. When Eric declined another drink, Chan went on, 'This kind of discrimination we can handle. The real difficulty arises in the business world. You see, the law says that we must not discriminate against the *bumiputera*. It so happens they are not—shall we say—as thrusting as the average Chinese businessman. They cannot compete with the Chinese. So the Government has evolved a solution to the problem of a possible Chinese domination of business in Malaysia.'

'Positive discrimination in their favour? But how does that work? If a *bumiputera* firm were subsidized—'

'That happens,' Chan interrupted. 'But that is not the main thrust of the legislation. They have hit upon a better solution. In every company registered in Malaysia, Chinese or Indian controlled, there must be *bumiputera* in senior positions: on the board of directors, in the senior management, holding positions of influence and control.'

'Must?'

'Exactly,' Chan said gravely. 'You will appreciate that this causes much resentment particularly where it is difficult to find men of quality among the available *bumis*.'

'So you'll occasionally employ figureheads?'

'And pay them more than they're worth,' Chan replied

drily. 'But that is no great problem. A business expense, one might say.'

'And you have *bumiputera* in your company?' Eric asked.

'Of course. And therein lies the problem. You see, trusting in your discretion, I will tell you. We chose what you would call a figurehead for Malaysia Mobile Berhad—the son of one of our Ministers. Unfortunately, he does not see himself as we see him. He believes he could do better than he is allowed to under our present company structure. Accordingly he—how do you say? Attempts to manipulate events.'

'Successfully?'

Chan permitted himself a dry chuckle. 'I said he attempts to do so.' He frowned, the smile quickly disappearing. 'However, he is always on the—how do the French say it?—the *qui vive*, watching for opportunities. And because of my position as Chairman, I am an obvious target.'

There was a short silence. Eric toyed with his food as Chan contemplated his half-filled brandy glass. There was a brooding quality about the silence, and Eric suspected that though Chan was dismissing the matter relatively lightly, it was nevertheless causing him some concern. It was perhaps wise to change the subject.

'So you—er—so you speak French, as well as English,' he ventured.

Chan nodded gravely. 'I speak a little French. I am more fluent in Japanese, Mandarin, Cantonese, Hakka, and of course, Malay.'

'You amaze me,' Eric said.

'No need. Remember my background. I was born into a Chinese merchant family, with Mandarin as our first language but also English-speaking, so I was early in life bilingual. But this was Singapore, and when the Japanese invaded and my parents died we were forced at school to learn and speak Japanese. I returned to English after the war, and spent some time with a French company in Indo-China before moving into Kuala Lumpur. One bends with the wind . . .' He looked at Eric keenly. 'But not always. Which is why I talk to you.'

'I don't understand.'

'I have no intention of relinquishing my Chairmanship of Malaysia Mobile Berhad.' His voice had taken on a steely edge.

'Is there a danger of that?'

Chan shrugged. 'There is a problem . . . which is being laid at my door. I do not intend it shall unseat me in favour of . . . a lesser man.'

Eric hesitated. 'What sort of problem?'

Chan shrugged. 'A matter of an unwise contract . . . and a sum of money is missing. It is not a large sum in Malaysia Mobile terms, but the fact it is missing is of importance. There is a member of my board who suggests it was all due to my negligence, and the trust I placed in an Englishman.'

Eric leaned back in his chair. 'The missing money . . . it was taken by an English employee of Malaysia Mobile?'

'It would seem so.' Chan rocked his head from side to side in doubt. 'But things are not always what they seem, is that not so? I feel sure the matter could be sorted out amicably enough if only I could speak to the man concerned. Perhaps you have heard of him. His name is Staughton. Harry Staughton.'

The impassive eyes were fixed on Eric suddenly. Eric shook his head. 'Can't say I've come across him.'

Chan reached inside his jacket. He drew out a photograph, and stared at it for a few seconds. He handed it to Eric. 'It's a good enough likeness.'

The photograph had been clipped from a larger one, showing a group of dark-suited men seated at a wide table, presumably taken in the boardroom of Malaysia Mobile Berhad in Kuala Lumpur. It showed the head and shoulders of a man in his early forties, with fair, crinkly hair and heavy eyebrows. His eyes seemed grey as far as Eric could make out from the colour photograph, and his mouth was wide, easy with its smile. He sported a thin moustache and his cheeks were lean, his features keen. There was a frosting of grey in his sideburns.

'I believe he's had business interests here in the North-East,' Chan said. 'And he was born in Sunderland.'

'A local lad.' Eric shook his head and offered the photograph back to Chan. He did not take it and, awkwardly, Eric retained it. 'I don't know him. But why can't you speak to him?'

Chan was silent for a few minutes, staring at his brandy, twisting it slowly in his hands, and ignoring the photograph Eric still held. 'Mr Staughton is a man of talents. He is intelligent, sharp in intellect. He is also a social animal. One trusts him easily . . .' Simon Chan paused thoughtfully, dwelling on the past. 'He rose to become Vice President and Charter Manager of our Singapore subsidiary, and was used by me to target the European and UK market. But then things seemed to go wrong. In his capacity as Charter Manager in Singapore he entered an unwise contract. It is of no great moment. But it means . . . I lose face.' He was silent for a little while. 'So far I have kept it quiet, away from my board. But there are suspicions . . . and pressures. If the information leaks out in an uncontrolled fashion, there is the possibility my *bumiputera* friend might seize the opportunity presented to him to . . . unsettle my position, shall we say? So discretion is important. I want no police involvement. I am sure Mr Staughton can explain . . .'

Eric began to understand. Behind Chan's impassive face was a controlled anger. The *bumiputera* 'figurehead' on his board wanted the Chairmanship, and saw this Staughton problem as a way of getting it. Chan wanted the inquiry kept under wraps, until he could deal with the problem, quietly, without publicity.

Simon Chan was staring at him. 'I enjoyed my discussion with your wife at Morcomb Estates. And the visit to Wallsend was . . . interesting. But if I may be frank, it did not come up to my expectations. There is much talk of what *will* be done, but the present evidence of real activity is slim. 'His eyes flickered away. 'The Teesside project also . . . Sir Henry Slocum is persuasive, but the deal is not closed yet. On the other hand, if my other business could be successfully, and discreetly concluded . . .'

When his eyes fixed again on Eric there was a glint in them. For a moment, Eric did not understand, and then when the meaning became clear he could hardly believe what Chan was suggesting.

He shook his head. 'Forgive me for my bluntness, but are you implying that if I were to take on an assignment from you this would in some way help you reach a decision about Morcomb Estates, and the Teesside project?'

'A deal with your wife's company depends upon the Teesside contract with Slocum,' Chan replied impassively. 'I have made no decision yet on the Teesside contract. And one *does* like to deal with friends . . . and colleagues. People one can trust, people who are discreet . . . and helpful.'

Eric smiled, bemused. 'Well, I'm happy enough to work for you on a retainer, but you don't need to dangle any other carrots in front of me, Mr Chan. My agreement to work for you will depend upon whether I feel I can be of assistance, not whether you'll give Morcomb Estates a distribution contract.' He stared again at the photograph. 'So, basically, I need to know—what do you want of me?'

'I have a board meeting of some importance in Kuala Lumpur in three weeks' time,' Chan said slowly. 'Before then, I require . . . it would be useful if I could have a conversation with Harry Staughton.'

'So why not have one?'

'Because Mr Staughton has made it difficult by disappearing, apparently without trace.'

Eric stared at him. 'Here, in England?'

'He was over here for the last eighteen months. We are no longer in contact with him—since the . . . unwise contract. And that is why I talk to you here, in the North-East. A man with your background . . . you could succeed where others have failed.'

'I don't understand.'

Simon Chan shrugged. 'You have had a career in the police. You tell me you have retained some of your . . . contacts, your network. I have already explained that I require discretion, and no formal police involvement. But I must find Staughton. I must have an explanation from him. I think you may well be able to help me—the man has a north-eastern background. He will be known in the area. Your contacts, your network . . .'

'You want me to find Harry Staughton for you.'

'Exactly. I feel sure a conversation with him will end my problems with my board. Just find him, Mr Ward.' Chan smiled thinly. 'Just find him. I will do the rest.'

3

Eric had not been completely honest with Simon Chan. When he had told him, somewhat deprecatingly, that he did a 'little' business in shipping, he had not been entirely accurate. Some three years previously Eric had picked up a few small Tyneside contracts, and these had effectively seeded themselves to the Wear and to Teesside. Shipping companies on Wearside and in Middlesbrough had begun to call upon his services and so Eric had brought into the firm a young legal executive, who was undertaking the specialized work for Eric. He was a bright young Tynesider, a Byker lad called Edward Elias: within a year, Eric had persuaded him to take advantage of the Law Society's entry arrangements to sit his examinations to become a solicitor. He should be qualifying within a year or so. Meanwhile, he spent most of his time on charterparty work and marine insurance.

Consequently, when Chan had given Eric a document file before he left the hotel, which turned out to contain papers relating to a ship called the *Arctic Queen*, Eric thought it sensible to hand the file over to Edward Elias. It would mean the papers would be scrutinized by someone who was dealing daily with shipping contracts—and besides, Eric was hitting a particularly busy time of the month, which called him to London for several days.

The first issue in London involved a hearing at the Court of Appeal: it meant he was held in the court for the better part of two days, time he could well have used to more profit, particularly since the appeal was rejected. And then there was the board meeting at Martin and Channing.

Leonard Channing presided at the board with his usual sharp tongue and acerbic wit. Now in his sixties, the chairman of Martin and Channing was a lean cold man, with thin humourless lips and sharp patrician features. His exterior was urbane, his manner smooth but he was tough and unprincipled. He enjoyed winning arguments, and detested losing them. When Morcomb Estates had become involved with the merchant bankers and Eric had brought the *Sea Dawn* affair to a successful conclusion,* it was Leonard Channing who had personally suggested Eric join the board. It was not because he valued Eric's presence, however: rather, he saw it as a way of keeping an eye on him. He had since regretted the decision: their clashes had not ended in Channing's favour. He had since never failed to make it clear that Eric's presence on the board should be regarded as temporary only: one slip, and Channing would dislodge him.

It was with a certain surprise, therefore, that Eric found Leonard Channing advancing on him at the conclusion of the board meeting, an affable smile on his thin lips.

'Eric, my dear boy . . . Do you think you could spare me a few minutes, in my room?'

Channing had a personal suite in the drab, elderly building that housed Martin and Channing. It consisted of an ante-room in which his personal secretary was installed among pastel shades, annual reports and Spy cartoons on the wall. Some of Channing's dislike of Eric seemed to have

* *Premium on Death.*

rubbed off on the personal secretary: she never deigned to speak to Eric other than to introduce him into the suite. This time it was not necessary, as Channing led him in, but her heavy eyebrows expressed disdain.

'Well, then, Eric,' Channing said with a sigh, 'can I offer you a drink of some kind? Whisky? Brandy? Gin?'

'A mineral water will be fine.'

Leonard Channing raised a supercilious eyebrow. 'Ah, of course, I was forgetting. You take very little alcohol.' He nodded to his personal secretary, hovering in the doorway, and silently she walked across to the drinks cabinet and poured for the two men. Channing smiled. 'How is your state of health these days, Eric?'

'No great problem,' Eric replied shortly.

'Good, good,' Channing said insincerely as he accepted the elegant, cut glass whisky tumbler, 'And . . . ah . . . business? You still defending the poor and homeless among us?'

'The practice is going well enough.'

Channing eyed him over the rim of his glass. 'Never could understand why you don't work for that wife of yours.'

Eric did not rise to the bait. Channing smiled thinly and sat down in the deep leather armchair opposite Eric. 'Ah well, that's not the only thing I don't understand about you, my boy. But then, we've been over all that before, haven't we?'

'Ever since the *Sea Dawn*,' Eric replied, not averse to putting in the odd barb himself. Channing's eyes glittered momentarily, then he laughed, a short barking sound.

'*Touché!* my friend. However, it's not that business I have in mind, asking you to have a chat with me here. Rather, it's the Salamander affair.* You seemed to think at the time you came out of that rather well.'

'That's for others to say,' Eric replied easily.

'The board at least, was grateful,' Channing said, but

* *The Salamander Chill.*

there was no warmth in his voice. 'However, in view of the claimed expertise in such company arbitraging matters it seemed to me you might usefully take up the cudgels once more on behalf of Martin and Channing.'

'I don't see myself as an expert in merger and acquisitions business,' Eric protested mildly.

'Who among us is, these days? You're too modest, my boy! And I'm getting too old for what is essentially a young man's business, all this wheeling and dealing.' He paused, eyeing Eric craftily. 'Tell me, have you heard of Artaros SA?'

Eric frowned. 'I think so. Isn't it a company we've been undertaking some business with?'

Leonard Channing nodded. 'That's right. We took some of the underwriting risk in the flotation of a new share issue for them. Artaros is an international company: it has subsidiaries in Bermuda, Singapore, Spain and England. As far as we were concerned, getting on the tombstone with regard to their UK share issue was a good risk—it's a sound, well-respected company, and its projections are well certified. However . . .'

'There's a problem, after all?'

Leonard Channing sipped at his whisky. 'You might say that. The flotation has attracted marauders—always a risk, but I didn't expect such attention on this occasion.'

'And you've been handling this one personally.'

Channing's eyes glittered. 'That's right.'

Eric looked at the mineral water sparkling in his glass. Channing had been handling Artaros personally because it satisfied his sense of power: with a problem looming, however, he would want to protect his back—by finding someone to shoulder the blame if things went wrong. Eric saw no reason why he should be designated as the scapegoat.

'A marauder, you say?'

'Exactly. The flotation has coincided with a hostile bid, from CI Iberica SA. They've already made an offer, and it could throw out of the window all the work we've done on the flotation. They're in it, of course, just to push up the price of the shares; chances are, once they've reached a share price ceiling, they'll sell out again, and make a killing without having to pay for the shares at all.'

It was a standard ploy, Eric knew. 'What's the size of their holding they've acquired at the moment?'

'Seven per cent. But it seems they're hoping to get as high as sixteen per cent by the weekend.'

Eric leaned back in his chair. 'Who's masterminding the bid? I don't know too much about Iberica.'

Leonard Channing put down his glass. His nostrils flared in patrician disdain as he enunciated the name carefully. 'Matthew Coleman—or Matt, as he is referred to by the vulgar Press.'

'The name's vaguely familiar . . .'

'Matthew Coleman is an American. He has quite a history. His business activities in the States have provoked allegations of tax and stock fraud, inside dealing, "concert parties" of the kind we saw in Salamander which involve illegal share price manipulation—and there've been some exposés, as our American friends say, of alleged links with organized crime.'

'Proved?'

'Not as such.' Channing sniffed. 'The bad news is that some two years ago he decided to move his operations from the States to Europe. He lives in Switzerland now. He's already made two successful raids. On the Bushnell-Nevada raid he's reputed to have walked away with twenty million.'

'And the bid for Artaros shares is his next step?'

'Until something better comes along. Maybe he's just keeping his hand in: Artaros isn't that big a company to interest Coleman overmuch. Pocket money only, in my view.'

'Is Artaros asking Martin and Channing to prepare a defence?'

'They're hoping we'll find some white knight to charge

to the rescue, or put out a portfolio which will undercut Coleman . . . or maybe even come up with a smear campaign that will warn shareholders away from the Iberica bid.' He paused, eyeing Eric carefully. 'God knows, there's enough dirt lying around on Coleman for the right man to pick up.'

'Mudslinging isn't my scene, Leonard.'

'A successful rearguard action on behalf of Artaros could make your name.'

'I've no desire to make anything of my name.' Eric smiled cynically. 'You don't fool me, Leonard. If a successful campaign against Iberica was easy, you'd be in there like a hungry fox. You'd love to go to the board—and the newspapers—as the saviour of Artaros. But you're not playing the hungry fox . . . more the nervous rabbit.'

Channing frowned, his glance hardening. He was not pleased with the simile.

'Offering it to me,' Eric continued, 'simply means you foresee problems, and if Coleman wins, I'll be the one with egg on my face.' He shook his head. 'No, thanks, Leonard. It's not for me.'

'Afraid of a challenge?' Channing asked silkily.

'No. Careful about any challenge you put on my plate as a gift.'

'The board might see fit to suggest you take on the business.'

'They can suggest. I'm a non-executive director. I hold no particular brief. They can ask me . . . but they can't tell me. There's a difference.'

'So I can't persuade you, Eric?'

Eric finished his drink and stood up. He looked down on the urbane chairman of Martin and Channing. 'Let's be honest with each other, Leonard. We dislike each other . . . though we also respect each other, I suspect. I've far too much respect for your native cunning to accept a commission from you of this kind. There's simply no way you could persuade me to do this . . . it would be like putting a pistol in my mouth with your finger on the trigger.'

'Picturesque,' Channing murmured, 'but I must admit it's a picture not without appeal. Ah, well, if I can't persuade you, Martin and Channing will just have to muddle through as best it can. Thank you, at least, for listening. Till the next board meeting, Eric.'

Eric was sure he had been right. Channing's motivations were obvious: he wanted a scapegoat. Even so, as he flew back to Newcastle Eric could not resist recasting in his mind the events surrounding the Salamander affair. It had been a tiring, but exciting time. And the Iberica raid on Artaros showed all the signs of being a similar battle of wits and money. He was almost tempted to take up Channing's challenge—but maybe Channing was relying on the fact that Eric found it difficult to resist such a challenge, even if the dice were loaded.

The car was waiting for him at Newcastle Airport. Anne was at Berwick, and Eric had to put in an appearance at the office the following day, so he drove to the flat, showered, and made an early night of it.

There was a backlog of mail to deal with when he arrived at the Quayside next morning, and three clients to see. They were relatively minor matters, and he was able to deal with them fairly quickly. Nevertheless, it was late afternoon before he found time to ring down to Edward Elias.

'Eddie? How are you getting on with the stuff Mr Chan gave me?'

'I've done some notes, Mr Ward. You want me to come up now?'

'I'll get some tea in.'

By the time the tea arrived, Elias was sitting in Eric's office with Chan's folder on the desk and a notepad on his knees.

'Well, then, Eddie, what have you got?'

Elias nodded his head and frowned, concentrating. 'It's not easy, Mr Ward, because the papers Mr Chan gave you are sort of not complete. You know, they give part of the picture, but not everything. There's some gaps that I don't understand . . .'

'Just let me know what you do have.'

'Well, all the documentation relates to a ship called the *Arctic Queen*. It was first purchased by Malaysia Mobile under a time charter.'

'How long?'

'The time charter was for twelve months, with an option to purchase at the end of the charter. That option was taken up three years ago.'

'Is there anything in the papers to suggest a reason for the purchase?' Eric asked.

'Not really. As an educated guess, I can suggest it was probably with a view to chartering onwards—Malaysia Mobile appear to be in the chartering business. Indeed, the signatory to the documentation is one J. H. Staughton, who is designated as Charter Manager.'

'He was also Vice President of the company.'

'So clearly he had authority to enter the transaction.'

'What were charter prices like around about that time?' Eric queried.

'Three years ago?' Elias wrinkled his nose in thought. 'They were just peaking, I think. They'd been rising internationally for some time, but they were just about to level off, as far as I recall.'

'Right. So what else have you got?'

'The rest of the documentation refers to a separate matter. I want to come back to the history of the *Arctic Queen* in a moment, if I may, sir. But to go on: the papers then show that the *Arctic Queen* was chartered under a similar deal to that under which it had been acquired by Malaysia Mobile.'

'You mean it was chartered onwards, with an option to buy? When was that?'

'Just one year later.'

'To whom?'

'To a company called Ocean Distribution Ltd.'

'UK registered?'

'Yes, Mr Ward, but the contract was entered into and the charterparty concluded in Singapore.'

'Does that raise a problem?' Eric asked.

'Not according to the documentation. The problem—or problems—seem to lie elsewhere. In the first instance, there's a copy of a certified cheque which appears to have been dishonoured.'

'Let's have a look.' Eric took the proffered cheque copy and scanned it. 'It's made out to Malaysia Mobile. Why has it bounced?'

'The notation suggests it's a forgery—a replica of another cheque, which had a different payee, and which was cashed.'

'Who was the other payee?'

'Nothing is noted, sir.'

But Eric could guess. The cheque photocopy in his hands was in the sum of £850,000. The deal had been struck by Harry Staughton as Charter Manager. Harry Staughton was missing, and Simon Chan had said there was a sum of money to be accounted for . . . not large in Malaysia Mobile terms, but . . . Large enough, Eric thought grimly.

'There would seem to be another issue, sir, if I may draw your attention to it.'

'Go on.'

'The papers aren't explicit. Nevertheless, it would seem, as far as I can make out, that the missing money is not the only issue between the two companies—Ocean Distribution and Malaysia Mobile.'

'What else are they quarrelling about?'

'The nature of the contract itself, it seems. The terms of the charterparty. But I can't offer an opinion because the documentation is scanty.'

'I see.' Eric thought for a little while. 'Would it be because the matter is still in a state of preparation by the lawyers?'

'I would think so. There's no record of a court appearance, and I've checked with London.'

Eric sighed. It didn't take him much further, but it did give him some background, at least. If he was to find Harry Staughton for Simon Chan, it was time to buy some legwork, use the network as Chan wanted. 'All right, Eddie, that's fine. I'm grateful—'

'There is something else, sir. I mentioned I'd like to return to it.'

'Yes? What is it?'

Elias scratched his head and leaned back in his chair. 'It's about the original purchase of the *Arctic Queen* by Malaysia Mobile, Mr Ward.'

'What about it?'

'Well, setting aside the fact that it was a bit unwise . . . with hindsight, at least, with freighting rates falling and charterparty prices going down, it was a bad time to buy. But there's something else. It relates to the *Arctic Queen* herself.'

'How do you mean?'

'As a matter of form I looked up Lloyd's and the register. It's almost automatic when you're dealing with charterparties . . .'

'What did you find?' Eric asked, puzzled.

'Nothing I can be quite certain of, sir.' Elias frowned. 'But there's something odd about the history of the *Arctic Queen*. It seems she went through a major refit some five years ago, and was used in the Pacific by the previous owners. There was litigation about her in New York—'

'Sounds as if she carries a jinx,' Eric said.

'The claim in court was that she was unseaworthy.'

'So?'

'That was *after* the refit, sir. And I can find nothing in the registration to suggest the problems—if there were problems—had been put right.'

Eric stared at Elias. The young man looked uncomfortable, aware he was guessing as a result of inadequate documentation, rather than coming up with hard facts. 'Are you suggesting,' Eric asked slowly, 'that Malaysia Mobile might have been sold a pup in the first place?"

"I think it's possible. I can't be sure. But it might be why they offloaded the vessel so quickly thereafter to Ocean Distribution. There's nothing in the papers to suggest the Ocean people are raising it as an issue—maybe it's not even come to their attention, or maybe the matter has been remedied. I don't know. But it does explain the early offloading by Malasyia Mobile.'

'Hmmm.' Eric thought for a while, musing, swinging in his chair. 'You say the original purchase by Malaysia Mobile took place in Singapore.'

'That's right. The Charter Manager was based there. The Ocean Distribution deal was also completed there.'

'When Malaysia Mobile was sold a pup—if they were sold a pup—who did they buy from?'

Elias consulted his notes. 'Ahhh . . . it was a subsidiary of an international shipping company. It was called . . . ah . . . Artaros SA.'

Eric thought about it for the rest of the day. He rang Anne to make sure she'd be home that evening, and then he took the car and drove back to Sedleigh Hall. The evening was grey, storm clouds hiding the hills as he drove northwards, and there was a spatter of rain on his windscreen. Across to his left he caught occasional flashes of lightning towards the coast and there was the distant growl of thunder, but nothing broke inland.

He reached Sedleigh Hall at eight, and went upstairs to take a shower. Anne would not be home for another hour so he got himself a drink and switched on the television. The inanity of the programme drove him to switch off after ten minutes, and then he sat in the twilit room, nursing his drink, thinking.

At last he rose, and picked up the phone. He dialled Leonard Channing's private number. The maid answered.

Channing was out: he'd be back at ten. She would take a message.

When Anne arrived they dined quietly. She was tired, and preoccupied with the results of her meeting in Berwick. He did not question her: he had other things on his mind. He was not certain he was doing the right thing.

The phone rang precisely at ten.

'Eric? You wanted to speak to me?'

'Thanks for ringing back so promptly, Leonard. I . . . I've been thinking over our conversation in your office.'

'The Iberica business?'

'That's right. I—er—I wonder whether I was a bit hasty. There are aspects of the thing I might find interesting.'

Leonard Channing was silent for a few moments. Then he chuckled. 'You mean you are contemplating taking the matter on, after all?'

'Where is the operation being masterminded from?'

'The managing director is a chap called Greg Bowles. He's based in Singapore. You'd have to work with him over there. I'd be along for the opening shots, of course, but then I've too much on my plate to be tied down to the Artaros-Iberica battle.'

'Yes. I understand that.'

'So are you prepared to reconsider, then?'

'I—I think so.'

Leonard Channing chuckled. He seemed amused, but there was an edge of triumphant relief in the sound also. 'Well, well, so I was right. You simply can't resist that sort of challenge, can you, dear boy? All right—you'll get the papers tomorrow, and my secretary will book us the flights immediately.'

When Eric replaced the phone Anne was staring at him. 'Do I gather from that conversation you'll be working closely with Leonard Channing again?'

'I suppose so.'

'Do you think that's wise, Eric?'

'I don't know,' he said. 'I really don't know.'

CHAPTER 2

1

They did not travel to Singapore together.

Leonard Channing had arranged to travel on the Tuesday, but consultations at the Appeal Court delayed Eric so he was unable to join Channing until the Thursday flight. He was more than a little relieved: he and Channing had little in common and he had not been looking forward to Leonard Channing's company on the long flight east.

They were both booked into the Westin Stamford hotel. When Eric arrived in the early evening a car was waiting for him at Changi Airport. It whisked him along the dual carriageway towards the glow of the city, brightly lit with its towering hotels, financial buildings and shopping centres. The car swung into the curving drive of the hotel and uniformed doormen were there to assist him as he got out. His luggage was already being attended to as he was directed up the steps.

The front desk in the wide reception area at the Westin Stamford was clearly expecting him and he was welcomed by name. There was a note waiting for him at reception from Leonard Channing, suggesting they met for dinner. When Eric went up to the thirtieth floor to shower and change he discovered that his room gave him a glittering view of the Singapore River, the War Memorial to those who died in the Japanese occupation, and the harbour itself crowded with shipping, dark against the moonlit sea. Eric unpacked quickly, took a shower and dressed. The room was cool from the air-conditioning but outside he knew the humidity would be high.

*

Channing was already seated in the restaurant. It had been a short cab drive from the hotel itself to Emerald Hill Road, and Channing had already begun to order—'just in case you were late, dear boy.'

Channing was in expansive mood. He had forsaken his normal, dark-suited appearance, and wore light slacks and a brightly coloured batik shirt. He was enthusiastic about the cuisine.

'Your first time in Singapore, Eric? I can recommend the *soto ayam* and the *tahu goreng*—use the spicy peanut sauce with it. And if you want something even spicier, try the *gado gado* salad.'

'I wasn't aware you were interested in Malaysian food,' Eric said.

'Don't jump to conclusions. I've been here two days acclimatizing.' Channing waved his fork in a grandiose gesture. 'I've revisited places I knew years ago, and done the tourist bit—Sentosa Island and the Occupation display; Jurong Bird Park; Bukit Timah Racecourse. And I've been sampling—Chinese, Indonesian—and tonight Malaysian food.' He grinned, more relaxed than Eric had ever seen him. 'And I'd advise you to get some lighter clothing. In this humidity you'll melt.'

Eric inspected the menu and ordered *beef rendang* and *satay*. Channing had already obtained a bottle of wine and suggested Eric join him. Eric accepted a glass. He waited while Channing went through the preliminaries, inquiring after his flight and his room. Then, when the food arrived, Eric asked, 'Have you fixed up anything with Artaros?'

'Ten tomorrow morning.'

Eric grunted and sipped his wine. 'You get three days to overcome jet-lag, I get none?'

'Should have come out with me, dear boy! And time presses. I must return to London on Sunday. You're booked too.'

'Thanks very much. We'll be meeting Bowles tomorrow, then?'

'That's it.' Channing observed the wine in his glass appreciatively. 'Australian. I've had worse . . . I had a brief conversation with Bowles on the phone yesterday. He's hopping mad about the Iberica bid.'

'Has there been any further movement on the shareholding?'

'Iberica's kept up the pressure. They've increased their holding to about twelve per cent already. It seems,' Channing said thoughtfully, 'our arbitraging friend Matt Coleman is serious. It might not be big league stuff for him, but he's pushing hard.'

'It may be the prelude to other and bigger things,' Eric suggested.

'You mean the Artaros attack is a sort of exploratory touch finder? Hmm . . . Could be. Once he's bloodied a few noses in this deal, he'll be more able to put frighteners on other companies in Europe.'

'Any sense of the timing in this one, Leonard?'

Leonard Channing frowned and shook his head. 'Not really. The bid is in, and Iberica are picking up the shares all right, but my guess is once Coleman's taken, maybe, a sixteen per cent holding for Iberica the price of Artaros stock will have rocketed enough for him to sell and run for cover with money in his fist.' He bared his teeth in a wolfish grimace. 'I sometimes think merchant banking was perhaps a little too quiet an option for me. Some of these attacks . . . they're really quite exciting.'

'From the sidelines,' Eric suggested. 'Don't think the piratical life can be anything other than dangerous.'

'I've no doubt about it. And I suppose in our business we can get the excitement, while avoiding most of the danger.'

'We're still central.'

'But playing with money belonging to the pirates and the victims. A better business position to take, don't you agree?' Channing smiled, wolfishly again. 'But, to extend the analogy, I have the distinct impression that if Greg Bowles of Artaros could only get his hands on our American friend Matt Coleman, walking the plank would be a certainty. As you'll discover tomorrow . . .'

The oil refineries that towered over the scattered islands of Singapore Harbour had made the Lion City the third biggest refining centre in the world. From the balcony of his room Eric enjoyed the panoramic view across the city: the sun was hot but the humidity was already high as he stood there, looking down on the immaculate greensward of the Padang and the Singapore Cricket Club.

The black air-conditioned limousine sent from Artaros collected Eric and Channing at the hotel at 9.30. They were driven swiftly into the city. Channing chattered enthusiastically about the concentration of banking interests, and the teeming port trade in Singapore. He was of the opinion that Martin and Channing should be looking more positively towards investment in what he had been told was known locally as the Crossroads of the World.

'It's also been described as a police state with carrots,' Eric suggested.

'A benevolent suppression—and why should they kick against the restrictions and constraints if their physical and economic well-being is so beautifully catered for? If that's what you mean by the carrots.'

They passed the Supreme Court and the Armenian Church and then the exotic street names flashed past: Sultan Gate, Jalan Kubor, Buffalo Road.

Asian Artaros Building was a twenty-storey, modern glass and concrete construction on the edge of the business sector. Glass doors soughed quietly, opening automatically at their approach: the air-conditioning within made Eric shiver briefly, in contrast to the humidity they'd experienced as they had stepped from the car.

Channing smiled thinly. 'In Singapore you put your coat on to go indoors.'

A dark-suited Eurasian girl welcomed them with a wide

smile: she issued them with security passes, then directed them towards the lift.

A polite young man met them at the lift which whisked them to the twentieth floor and the directors' suite of offices. They came out into what appeared to be a large marble-floored hall, whose windows gave a panoramic view of the Lion City and the Singapore River. A smiling, white-shirted Singaporean offered them cold drinks and invited them to look at the view. 'It is all here, gentlemen,' he said. 'Modern skyscrapers, old Chinese shop houses, mosques, bazaars and back lanes. A marriage of past and future. Mr Bowles will be with you shortly.'

He remained with them for a few minutes, pointing out to them the landmarks visible from the windows: the Merlion Park, Parliament House and the landing site where Sir Stamford Raffles had first stepped ashore in 1819. 'There is a statue there of Raffles,' he explained, 'erected on the bank of the Singapore River, but it is a copy. The original stands in front of the Victoria Theatre.'

A voice cut in from behind them. 'Thank you, Lee . . . Gentlemen, I'm sorry I'm a little late.'

Greg Bowles was immensely tall. Eric calculated he was at least six feet four, but he stooped slightly, as though conscious of his height, so he could have been taller. He wore a white, short-sleeved shirt, dark tie, and dark slacks. He was perhaps fifty years of age, but clearly maintained a fitness regime for he showed no paunch, his body was lean and he moved lightly, almost catlike in his tread. His features were strong, accustomed to obedience: a powerful hooked nose, dark eyes and eyebrows, but his hair, which he wore short cropped, was a startling white. His handshake was searching, testing in its strength as though he was weighing up opposition, and his voice was deep and resonant. His tones were clipped, as the introductions were made, and Eric guessed he would have little time for small talk. He would not be a sociable animal: his life would revolve around business.

He waved them towards some easy chairs situated across the room, against the windows. 'We can talk there. I'm grateful for your visit. A good flight out, I trust.' He did not wait for a reply. 'The Iberica attack needs to be handled swiftly.'

Eric was taken aback by the almost aggressive move to immediate business talk. It smacked of obsession and he was silent for a moment. Channing responded more quickly.

'I gather they're still buying in,' Leonard Channing said.

'That bastard Coleman . . . His tactics are clear. Once he's got a major stake the prices will move even higher than the one he's offering. Then he'll get out quickly.'

'And after that, a slump?' Eric asked.

Bowles's dark eyes dwelled on him briefly. 'Highly likely. And other reactions. It'll damage us in the market-place. We'll be left licking wounds. And when you're wounded, other sharks gather.'

'You'd anticipate other hostile bids?'

'Inevitably.'

Leonard Channing pursed his lips thoughtfully. 'Tactically, we've come armed with a number of suggestions—'

'I want Coleman.'

Bowles's interruption was vehement. He glared at Channing with a cold commitment that surprised the merchant banker. Channing faltered. 'I'm not certain—'

'I want him. This is more than a raid. It's personal. Both ways.'

After a short silence, Eric said, 'I think you'll have to explain that.'

Greg Bowles stared at him, his mouth twisted slightly as though he disliked even mentioning the existence of Matt Coleman. 'I've had dealings with the bastard,' he said viciously.

'You mean negotiations have gone on between Artaros and Iberica before this?'

Bowles shook his head. 'No. The details needn't concern

you. Let's just say that Coleman and I almost entered a business association once. It fell through. There was bitterness on both sides.'

'This was here in Singapore?'

'No. In the States. Some years ago.'

Eric frowned. 'And you think the residue of . . . feelings developed then are behind the Iberica raid on Artaros?'

'I'm certain of it,' Bowles snapped. 'Coleman is in trouble in the States. That's why he's moved into Europe. But he has some way to go yet. He's got to set up the kind of base he had in New Jersey. It takes time. That's why he's going for us at Artaros. It's seed corn money for him. The profits he'll make—while spending little—will finance him for bigger deals in Europe. This is just a sideline.'

'But why Artaros?'

'Because he hates my guts. And if he can do some business and nail me to the wall at the same time, he'll jump at the chance.'

Eric felt vaguely uncomfortable. There was a vehemence and underlying viciousness to Bowles's views that disturbed him. Bowles's attitude towards Coleman lacked balance. It was as though the man believed the quarrel he and Coleman had had years ago was serious enough to lead to a personal vendetta.

'What did you mean when you said you want him?' he asked.

Greg Bowles was still, his fingers linked together as he squeezed them, his hands white-knuckled. 'Simply that. Mr Ward, we'd better be clear about one thing. I think we can guess what Coleman's tactics will be. They're classic. Buy in, push prices up, get out when the raid's achieved its objective. But we can't be sure. Coleman and I have a personal quarrel. Could be he'll want more than just a raid.'

'Such as?'

'Wipe me out.'

'But—'

'If this raid is mishandled at our end, my arse could be on the line. That's why I want Coleman—before he gets me.'

Eric felt uncomfortable. He glanced at Leonard Channing, but the merchant banker was giving nothing away, a frozen half-smile on his face, emphasizing the distance he was placing between himself and the turn of the conversation. Channing looked at Eric, clearly expecting him to continue. He was taking a back seat in a situation which he clearly regarded as being too intense.

'You know something of Coleman in the States?' Bowles queried.

'You mean his business activities there? I gather there have been allegations of tax and stock fraud,' Eric replied.

'Right. But there's more than that. He's got links with organized crime. There's a tie-in with the Rocco family who own large holdings in Las Vegas. The Roccos tried to take a larger stake in some casinos in Atlantic City—the New Jersey authorities had to crack down. Coleman was in on that. On the wrong side.'

'I'm not clear—'

'The only way to deal with a man like Coleman is to fight fire with fire. I got to know him well. Before our deal fell through I learned a lot about him. He's vulnerable. I want his belly slit.'

Channing stirred but said nothing.

Eric hesitated. 'Look, you're indulging in rather colourful remarks, Mr Bowles, but I'm not clear what you're suggesting. This is a fairly simple—albeit serious—matter of a hostile bid from Iberica, a corporate raid of the kind we've often seen of recent years in Europe. Now the strategy—'

'Normal strategies won't work. I know Coleman. He's tough, but he's got a soft underbelly like everyone else. And his is exposed through the Rocco dealings. The way to nail Coleman, and destroy his raid on Artaros, is to make him concentrate elsewhere. Defend, instead of attack.'

'And just how do you propose we do that?' Eric asked.

'Highlight the allegations about his past.'

'In an attempt to shake off his unwanted attentions?' Channing mused. 'It's original.'

Eric was silent. Bowles was too angry, too vicious in his assessment for it to make sense to him. He watched the managing director of Artaros as he expounded upon his theme. The man was almost beside himself with a cold, barely suppressed rage. His commitment to raise a strong defence against the Iberica raid was clear, but his tactics were obviously going to be aggressive, and in a sense unconnected with the raid itself. 'A Press assault is the first step,' he was saying. 'I'll want you to seed stories about the Rocco connection, place items about the tax and stock fraud investigations, drop hints about insider dealing. Coleman's a womanizer, too. I've got sources on that.' He paused, his mouth hard as something stirred in his mind, unpleasant memories or ancient hurts. 'I want it published. Then there's the New York "concert party" over the Chicago stockyard deal. I want a campaign mounted.'

'I'm not sure these tactics—'

'I want all the Artaros shareholders to be aware that if they sell to this man they'll be dealing with someone who's nothing but a crook.' Bowles glared fiercely at Eric. 'I want him exposed. Stripped naked.'

'Have you thought of the laws of libel?' Eric asked quietly.

Bowles managed a smile. It was thin, vicious, and lacking in humour. 'I'm no innocent in the corporate or legal jungle, Mr Ward. I don't expose myself unnecessarily. Or without due care. I've got documentation prepared. It's been cleared by Artaros lawyers. It'll form the basis of the campaign I want you to spearhead.'

'It's not exactly what we had in mind—'

'But I'm sure Eric will handle it with discretion,' Channing interrupted smoothly. 'An interesting approach . . . and he is an experienced lawyer, as I think I told you, Bowles.'

Greg Bowles grunted. He turned his head, gestured to the young Singaporean, who came forward with a document file. He handed it to Bowles, inclining slightly from the hips. Bowles thrust the file into Eric's hands.

'You'll find supporting stuff in there. Take a look at it. I have another appointment now, but if you hang on here, reading the file, I'll be able to join you for lunch. We'll eat here.'

'Well—er—' Leonard Channing was rising smoothly to his feet. 'I fear I'll have to forgo the pleasure, Mr Bowles. I also have another appointment, so I'll leave this with Eric—he'll be handling the matter anyway.'

Angrily Eric glared at Channing. 'You won't be joining us at lunch?'

'No.' Channing smiled. 'But I'll see you back at the Westin Stamford, and we'll be able to talk as we fly home together, of course.' He extended his hand to Bowles. 'A pleasure, sir. Eric will bring me up to date. But I have every confidence that you are placing the matter in good hands.'

As he left, Eric felt anger stirring his blood. Channing was transparent: he had come over expecting to play the senior role in the Iberica business, with Eric doing the work while he took the credit, but now he was scared off, concerned about the way in which Bowles wanted the matter handled. Eric was certain of that.

Moreover, it left the whole matter clearly in Eric's hands—and that would suit Channing. If anyone was damaged by this business, it would be Eric, not Channing.

And yet, in spite of himself, Eric was curious. Bowles seemed to be over-reacting to a personal situation, and though he could be right in his summing up of Coleman, it could be an obsessive over-assessment and in any case it was still a dangerous road to take. Perhaps the documentation Bowles had provided could be used, however, even if the tactics were dangerous.

'I'll have a look at this,' he said as Channing disappeared.

'It's instructive,' Bowles said sharply. 'I'll be back here about twelve.'

Greg Bowles had clearly done his homework. The document file contained a mass of information which concentrated on Coleman's business activities in the States. There was a detailed breakdown of the cases of tax and stock fraud, with annotations of the probable 'deals' struck between Coleman and the Government. Coleman's activities with the Rocco family were also detailed, though Eric saw no primary sources identified, so there could be some problems there. There was a list of European companies in which Coleman had declared an interest, together with an assessment and analysis of the possible strategies Coleman might adopt. There was also a long list of the corporate raids he had made during the previous five years, and details of the funding sources he had used.

Eric read the material with interest. The time passed swiftly. He was brought coffee and a cold drink while he worked, but the staff remained at a discreet distance and did not interrupt him. He was a little surprised when Greg Bowles suddenly returned: he glanced at his watch. He had been reading the material for almost two hours.

'Well?' Bowles snapped.

'Interesting.'

'Is that all you have to say?'

Eric shrugged. 'I'll need to check some of your sources. As for the unsourced material I would recommend not using it. To put out Press leaks on that stuff would be dangerous—it could backfire with a libel suit.'

'If Coleman found out who pushed it out.'

'I assume,' Eric replied drily, 'his investigatory powers are as well resourced as yours.'

'Humph. Come on, let's eat.'

They passed out of the large room to a smaller dining-room which overlooked the city and Fort Canning. The tablecloth was rich white damask, the cutlery silver. A white-coated waiter served them with a selection of Chinese dishes as they discussed tactics.

Bowles was committed to a confrontational approach. Eric was more cautious, identifying only those particular issues which had been adjudicated on—they could safely be used in a Press campaign because they were in the public arena.

'But some of the other stuff is damaging!'

'True. But if it won't stand up in a court of law, in a libel suit, you shouldn't use it. However, there is one other thing . . .'

'Yes?'

'There's mention of a company called North Lagoon, Inc. It appears to have funded some of the raids Coleman made three years ago.'

'What about it?'

'Do you have any details?'

'Only what's in the file. Why?'

Eric shook his head. 'I'm not sure. But maybe I'll take a closer look at that myself. I've come across the name elsewhere, in some other capacity . . .'

He went on to discuss the proposed strategy that Martin and Channing were recommending to fight off the raid from Coleman. Bowles was unimpressed. He listened, but finally insisted that while he had no objection to any strategy being used to hurt Coleman and Iberica, he still wanted a Press smear campaign as a major effort with first priority. It was, in his view, the only way to beat Coleman.

At the conclusion of lunch Bowles offered Eric a drink. Eric accepted a brandy and soda; Bowles took a gin sling. With the business over he seemed to relax a little, his vendetta with Matt Coleman receded into the background and some of the nervous tension disappeared. He remained curt in his responses, but as he talked about the growth of Artaros and the part he had played in it he became less tense, and more friendly. Yet Eric detected a commitment lying just below the surface all the time: the sheen of relaxation could be wiped away in a moment. The man lived for his work, and had no time for other interests.

Eric wondered if he was married.

'So this is your first visit to South-East Asia, Ward?'

'That's right. Though oddly enough, I've recently agreed to act for a company in Kuala Lumpur.'

'Is that right? Who?'

'Malaysia Mobile Berhad. You've come across them, I believe.'

'Why do you say that?'

Eric smiled and sipped his iced brandy. 'Haven't you had dealings with them?'

Greg Bowles stared at Eric. Some of the relaxation was seeping from his body: he sat more stiffly, there was a tension back in the corners of his mouth and when he replied it was in a guarded tone. 'Malaysia Mobile . . . Yes, we've had dealings with them. They have shipping interests. Their managing director—'

'Simon Chan.'

'Chan. That's right. I've met him.' He paused, eyeing Eric carefully. 'What's your business with them?'

Eric shrugged. 'Nothing very much. Some private work. But I believe . . . didn't you sell them one of your ships a few years back? The *Arctic Queen*?'

There was a short silence. Bowles lowered his eyes, staring at his gin sling. He seemed to be weighing something up in his mind before he replied. Then he grunted. 'The *Arctic Queen*. Huh! I remember. I always thought, when we held that rustbucket, it was a crazy name for a ship plying in Pacific waters and the Indian Ocean.'

'Rustbucket?'

Greg Bowles stared coldly at Eric, meeting his glance almost contemptuously. 'We've had better ships.'

'But you sold her to Malaysia Mobile at a good price?'

'For considerably more than she was worth.'

Eric stared at him in surprise. The admission was an odd one, and there was a bitterness in Bowles's tone that was out of place when describing a deal in which he must have come out best. 'Did Simon Chan ever complain about the price?'

Bowles shook his head. 'Didn't deal with Chan, nor with Malaysia Mobile direct. It was completed through International Charters—a guy called Les Reynolds. Bastard! Served them right.'

'I don't understand.'

Bowles's glance had become vague and unseeing almost as though he was thinking of other things, unable to concentrate on the matter in hand. He shrugged non-committally. 'People think you're a fool. Think you were born yesterday. Reynolds thought he knew better than some of us who were in the front line of the business. He arranged a time charter for Malaysia Mobile. There was an option to purchase, could be taken up after twelve months. Freight charges were still rising—but more than a few of us knew the situation was peaking. Reynolds thought he knew better.'

'They took up the option on his advice?'

'I wouldn't know what advice they took. But they bought the *Arctic Queen*. They thought they were on to a good thing.'

'Whereas in fact you were offloading a liability,' Eric said quietly.

Bowles sneered openly. 'As a lawyer, Ward, you should know there's a time-honoured phrase: *Caveat emptor*.'

'Let the buyer beware . . . I know it. But if the ship wasn't seaworthy . . .'

Bowles stared at his glass. He hardly appeared to have heard Eric; he gave the impression that his mind was drifting again, thinking of other things, concentrating on other problems. Eric was surprised: the man was so sharply committed to his business that to lose touch momentarily like this was odd. Bowles struggled back. 'What was that?' he demanded.

Eric shook his head. 'You sold them what you described

to me as a rustbucket, through International Charters. As you say, *caveat emptor*. But where did Harry Staughton fit in to all this?'

'*Harry Staughton?*' The question seemed to stupefy Greg Bowles. There was a sudden greyness around his mouth, a quick nervousness in his eyes. 'That bastard?'

Eric stared, surprised at the reaction. After a moment he asked, 'Did you have dealings with him? Personally, I mean?'

'Personally?' Bowles's features tightened, the skin around his mouth seeming to become almost yellow, his eyes glazing momentarily. 'Staughton? Who told you about him?' He leaned forward angrily. 'What do you know about Staughton? Who's been talking to you about him?'

Eric was shaken by the virulent hatred in the man's voice. 'No one's been talking to me about him. I . . . I know he was Charter Manager here in Singapore, working for Malaysia Mobile. I'd assumed . . . I mean, as Charter Manager, wouldn't he have negotiated the charter with you, and the subsequent purchase?'

'I told you,' Bowles said harshly. 'Reynolds negotiated it.'

Eric waited, as Bowles glared moodily at his glass. The man was disturbed, clearly, and he had lost the control he had exhibited throughout their earlier conversation, in spite of his dislike for Matt Coleman. Now he struggled to regain that control as he twirled his glass between his fingers.

'As I said, Reynolds negotiated both charter and later purchase, but yes, Staughton was behind it.' He paused, breathing hard, still searching for control. He grunted unpleasantly. 'Like Reynolds, he thought he could do well for himself. He didn't realize the bottom was falling out of the market.'

'So you agreed an inflated price for the *Arctic Queen*?'

'It's not up to me to point out to fools the errors of their ways.' Bowles chewed at his lip. 'Both those idiots thought they were pulling a fast one. But not over me, Ward, not over me . . .'

It sounded, oddly enough, almost as though he was trying to persuade himself of the fact.

'You've not seen anything of Staughton since he left Singapore . . . or heard anything of him?'

Greg Bowles raised his head. He didn't want to receive the question, for some odd reason. Nor did he want to reply. Yet there was a struggling curiosity in his glance as he stared hard at Eric, searching for signs of dissembling, wanting to strip away any subterfuges that might lie there. 'Seen him? No, I've not seen him since he left. Heard of him?' For a moment the hints of an explosion seethed beneath the surface control of the man. They were suppressed. 'Heard of him? Don't want to. Why should I? He was a *little* man—smooth, charming, elegant, persuasive, but believe me, at base he was nothing but a cheap, little, small-hearted man. A thief in the night, and a liar.'

'I'm not sure—'

'In my view, for what it's worth, the man was an unprincipled crook. He'd have skinned his grandmother if he thought there was a market for ancient hides. On the surface, he could be a good companion. But I think there was something rotten about him, a worm in the apple of his character. I suspect he was actually incapable of playing a straight deal—there was no fun in it for him, no thrill. He wasn't a businessman. He was nothing more than a thief. And there are all kinds of theft . . .' He paused, his eyes narrowed as he stared into space ahead of him. Then he turned his head. Bowles's glance was veiled and thoughtful as he looked at Eric. 'What's your interest in him, Ward?'

Eric shook his head. 'He's just a name that's come up.'

'In what context?'

'In discussions with Simon Chan.'

'He employed him.'

'That's right,' Eric agreed. 'But the discussions . . . they were of no importance. No real importance.'

'I bet,' Bowles said disbelievingly. 'I bet.'

He seemed to be struggling with himself, and when the words finally were uttered they were dragged out, reluctantly, unwillingly. 'Staughton was a menace—crooked as they come, though I guess Malaysia Mobile never knew that. As I didn't, not at that time.' He paused, breathing irregularly as his chest seemed to tighten. 'If you do come across him at all . . . if you do pick up any information . . . I'd like to hear.' Bowles hesitated, fighting for the right words, and the hand that held his gin glass shook slightly. 'Yes, I'd like to hear. You see, I owe that man. I owe Harry Staughton.'

He looked at Eric coldly, recovering his poise and bringing the old steel back into his voice. 'I owe him . . . and it's a debt I'd like to repay.'

2

Eric was right in his understanding of Channing's position. Whatever enthusiasm Channing might have had originally to be involved in the Iberica defence for Artaros, it had rapidly evaporated when he realized it could develop into a mud-slinging attack by Bowles's company. Such dirty work was best left to Eric, who could bear the blame if things went wrong.

Eric himself had severe reservations about the procedures Bowles was insisting upon. On the other hand, having seen the documentation provided by Bowles, he realized there was certainly information there which should be transmitted to holders of Artaros stock: the large investors might be wary of dealing with a man of Coleman's shady reputation.

The long flight back left him exhausted: two such flights within a week was a bad enough problem since he usually had a recurrence of pain in his eyes when flying; to be stuck for over twelve hours with Leonard Channing was a further test of his stamina.

He was glad to get home.

'So how are you going to handle it?' Anne asked as they walked on the hills above Sedleigh Hall.

'The documentation looks sound, but I'd like a further check made. Phil Cooper's the obvious choice.'

'Your financial journalist friend. You think he'll come up with anything useful?'

'His contacts are wide.' Eric stopped, placed his back against a craggy outcrop and folded his arms. Anne stood beside him, leaning lightly against his shoulder, making the light contact that they both enjoyed. Below them the hill dropped green in the afternoon sun, and the roofs of Sedleigh Hall gleamed redly, its walls a warm sandstone colour where the sunlight struck them. 'I sometimes wonder why I bother, when I've all this to come back to.'

'I could always pull out our investments in Martin and Channing.' Anne hesitated. 'You could come off the board then. And if you worked with Morcomb Estates there'd be no need to go chasing off to London so often.'

He made no reply. She probably didn't expect him to—she knew his views about working for her company. 'Ah, it's probably just a reaction to my flight to Singapore.'

'Most probably,' she replied quietly, but there was a hint of frustration in her tone.

Phil Cooper stood over six feet and was built like a bull. He wore a dark blue jacket that seemed to be coming apart at the seams as his body strained to escape from its constaints. A square-built man, he had ice-blue eyes, chunky features and pitted cheeks; he had recently taken to sporting a moustache which contrasted with his sandy hair in a curious fashion, its whiteness emphasizing his tan, and partly cloaking the width of his smile. There were occasions when he deliberately played the buffoon but it was always with a reason: his general air of insouciance was a cultivated one, and his devil-may-care attitude was underlined by a professional seriousness that made him widely respected in financial journalism.

His weakness was that he loved intrigue, and his dealings with Eric had left him with an appetite for more, not least because he had several times succeeded in obtaining leads on stories that he had been able to break in the financial press.

He was able, trustworthy, and Eric liked him.

'So,' he said as he sat down uncomfortably, squeezing awkwardly behind the table in front of the narrow bench seat in the pub off the Strand. 'Back in the Smoke again?'

'Just for a few days,' Eric replied. 'Drink?'

'Whisky. Large. It's been a trying day.' He waited while Eric called an order at the bar. 'Martin and Channing business?'

'Right.'

'That's why you wanted to see me?'

'Always pleased to see you, Phil.'

'Likewise. But . . . I hear you're just back from Singapore.'

'News travels fast.'

'The wonders of modern telecommunications. But gossip flies even faster. I understand you're tied in with Artaros and their defence against CI Iberica.'

'You're well informed.'

'And that's why you invited me for a drink.'

'Sharp as a needle,' Eric said. 'What do you know about the character behind Iberica's bid?'

Cooper grimaced. 'Matt Coleman? Tough cookie, as they say. And rough too, if rumour has it right. He's been known to play the rules, but only rarely—he'd rather use a blunderbuss than a poignard—creates more blood. Though I gather he's not been averse to the odd knife between the ribs, for all that. But, well, let's just say he can be a . . . committed man.'

'I've got some documentation I'd like you to check out for me.'

'Indeed . . .' Cooper sipped his whisky, considering. 'Off the record stuff, of course.'

'Of course. In the main. But . . .'

There was a long pause. Cooper frowned. 'Not your usual scene, Eric. Am I right in thinking you're saying nothing . . . or that you're saying leakage in the newspapers would not destroy our confidence in each other . . .'

'Provided it's not attributable.'

Cooper placed a mocking, massive hand on his chest. 'A journalist's sources. But like I said, this isn't your . . . usual *modus operandi.*'

'Let's say I have a . . . forceful client.'

'Hmm. Greg Bowles, I would guess. Is that the documentation?'

Eric pushed the file across to him. The financial journalist opened it and skimmed through a few pages quickly. He whistled. 'Thorough stuff, this. I'll need to go through it carefully, and it may be I've got some leads . . .' He paused, closed the file and looked at Eric, a dancing, excited gleam in his ice-blue eyes. 'He wants a Press campaign, that's it, isn't it? Bowles wants to put the skids under Iberica with style.'

'And vigour.'

'I bet. Well, I'll certainly do some chasing. And you know—' the excitement grew, and Cooper chuckled—'you may well get the chance to see me in real action.'

'How do you mean?'

Cooper shook his head. 'You've never met this guy Coleman?'

'No.'

'I think I'm going to remedy that situation.' Cooper drained his glass and stood up, to struggle his way to the bar. 'The fact is, Coleman's called a Press conference for the financial journalists among us. The idea he has, I'm sure, is to put more pressure on Artaros by making some noise about his bid. Now, it could backfire.'

'How do you mean?'

Cooper grinned. 'If I can get confirmation on this stuff you've given me, we'll get some headlines for Greg Bowles. Why not come along and see Big Phil in action? Ever seen a bull elephant on the rampage?'

A special room had been booked at the London Hilton. There were some twelve journalists present, including Phil Cooper, and although several looked curiously at Eric—for they all seemed to know each other—they made no inquiries. The fact he was with Cooper was enough to satisfy them. He was seen as a Cooper contact, and they did not interfere.

The morning was sunny. The trees in Hyde Park were in full leaf, and the sound of traffic roaring around the park itself was muted here in the hotel. A small dais had been raised at the far end of the room; soft drinks had been placed on the tables, but a uniformed waiter stood just inside the door taking orders for harder stuff. All the journalists took advantage of the offer; Eric himself was content with an orange juice.

He had phoned Anne to say he'd been delayed in London: the chance to meet Matt Coleman face to face had been too good to miss. And although Cooper had not been in touch since Eric had given him the documentation two days ago, there was an air of suppressed excitement about the big man when they entered the Hilton that made Eric guess Cooper was more than satisfied with what he had managed to confirm.

When Coleman finally made his appearance, some seven minutes after the appointed time, Eric was somewhat surprised. Coleman had a big reputation, and Eric had expected a big man. In fact, Matt Coleman was short, slim, well-groomed and urbane. He had a long, lugubrious face and a sallow complexion; his hands were narrow and nervous, but his eyes were calm. He exuded an air of confidence, and the story he had to tell was smoothly presented by his aides with the assistance of a video display and some charts.

The journalists sat quietly with their drinks in front of them on the green cloth-covered tables, and listened respectfully. Coleman sat back as a fresh-faced young man in a brown suit explained in a Boston accent the history of CI Iberica and its European intentions. The video presentation was slick, if not terribly informative as far as Eric was concerned, and the statements of the man who followed, though they concentrated upon the Iberica bid for Artaros stock, were curiously muted.

The reason became apparent when he ended, and Coleman stood up.

However cool his appearance, his voice was vibrant and strong.

'So much for background, gentlemen,' he stated. 'Some of it will be familiar to you. But let's get down to the reasons why you're here. You want to know what my intentions are, and what my strategy may be, with regard to the Artaros bid. So let it be clear—I'm prepared to talk on both. Moreover, I'm dead serious in my intentions. This is not a corporate raid. I'm not seeking to will-o'-the-wisp in and out again. Whatever you might have heard or read about me, I promise you, this bid is an attempt—which will be successful, believe me—to take over a weak and ailing management and transform a company that has lost its direction into one which will be profitable for staff and shareholders.'

'Lying bastard,' Cooper whispered, with a lopsided grin.

Eric listened while Coleman expounded upon his theme. This was no financial shark, no arbitraging raid: Coleman and Iberica were seeking a strong foothold in the European market and the way forward was to buy into a respected company which was staggering and out of direction. With the right stock-holding, and the right managerial direction, all could be saved. He had every confidence that he would obtain sufficient of the stock to take over the running of the company, and he had every confidence that the stockholders would benefit from his intervention. This was the message he was transmitting to them, and which he wished transmitted to the holders of Artaros stock.

The journalists scribbled. Phil Cooper did not.

When Coleman finished there was a quick flurry of questions, mainly concerned with detail regarding prices, financing, price/earnings ratios and capital gearing. Coleman answered the questions personally, and with confidence. Cooper sat with his hands folded, waiting for his moment.

The questions began to fade, and Coleman looked around, satisfied. 'Well, if there's nothing else—'

Phil Cooper stood up, fleshy hands on the table in front of him. 'A slick presentation, Mr Coleman. But one you've used in the States, I believe.'

Coleman raised an elegant eyebrow. 'Mr—'

'Cooper. My point is, the bullshit you've been serving us here only reflects the kind of stuff you've ladled out on at least three occasions back home. In other words, have you *ever* admitted that all you're doing is making a corporate raid?'

'I'm not sure I understand what you're driving at, Mr Cooper,' Coleman said easily. 'I've given some sincere statements out today about my reasons for the Artaros intervention. It's nothing to do with corporate raids. It's about taking an ailing operation—'

'Leopards don't change spots, Mr Coleman. You've said it all before. And pulled out once the megabucks rolled in.'

Coleman smiled: his teeth were even, white and predatory. 'Let's not look backwards, my friend. Motives change, of course, when the stakes are raised higher. But I can assure you—'

'Can you assure me that the tax fraud issues you were involved in back in the States are now over and done with?'

The fresh-faced young aide straightened in his seat. The pause, before Coleman spoke, was short. 'There are no Government writs out against me.'

'Including stock fraud?'

'I repeat, there are no Government—'

'And insider trading in Atlantic City?'

'Mr Cooper—'

'And what about the Chicago stockyard "concert party"?' Cooper persisted.

Coleman's lips thinned. He fixed Cooper with a cold stare, as the journalists in front of Cooper glanced back, feeling a change in the atmosphere in the room. 'I'm not certain what you're trying to say, Cooper. And none of it is germane to this conference.'

'On the contrary,' Cooper replied forcefully. 'You've been giving us a lot of rubbish about how clean your intentions are with regard to Artaros, but I think stockholders have a right to know whether they'll be dealing with someone whose activities back in the States have been the subject of Government investigation.'

The fresh-faced young aide leaned forward. 'Let's get something clear here. Any statements made that are libellous—'

Coleman silenced him with a gesture. 'Mr Cooper is right,' he said coldly. 'Stockholders have that right. And I've already given the assurance—'

'That no writs are out against you, I understand that,' Cooper interrupted. 'But what about Government investigations?'

The thin smile on Coleman's face was little more than a sneer. 'The US Government has seen fit to pursue a vendetta against me for some years. They are backed by powerful financial interests who see me as a threat and they have tried to smear by innuendo my legitimate financial activities—but unsuccessfully. If they choose to continue burrowing their noses into my affairs—carrying on investigations—that's nothing to do with me. I can't stop that.

Small, petty men, with reasons of their own which may be tainted with corruption . . .'

'So you don't discount the fact you may well still be the subject of investigation?' Cooper snapped.

There was a short silence. At last Coleman said icily, 'I am aware of no investigation.'

'So the Atlantic City casino business has all blown over? And the link with Corey Investments and the billion dollar fraudulent tax loss scandal has been cleared?'

'What the hell are you talking about? I was never linked with Corey.'

'Do you mean not yet?' Cooper asked sarcastically.

'Cooper—'

'The Coleman connection is on file.'

'Not the *Matt* Coleman connection,' the arbitrageur snapped. 'My brother's name was linked—he did plead guilty to one charge and that's on the record. He paid a fine. But I was not personally involved with Corey.'

'Your brother wasn't fronting for you?'

'I resent that. My brother is his own man. He has his own business interests. He's still in the States—'

'In jail?'

Coleman was silent for a few moments. 'I think that's enough,' he grated.

'And then there's the Roccos. Just exactly what is your link with them, Mr Coleman? And could you assure the flower of the British financial Press gathered here today that the funding of your . . . ah . . . enterprises here in Europe has nothing to do with that family connection? A connection, I understand, that is the subject of much comment in the States?'

Coleman leaned forward, knuckles on the table in front of him. The vibrancy of his voice had been replaced with a harsh, grating note. 'I have been accustomed to muck-raking journalistic activity in the States; I did not expect to receive such treatment here. I'm not certain about your motivation, Mr Cooper, but I am certain that you'd better get your facts right or start looking for another job. You'll never last the pace. There is no connection between the Rocco family and myself; there is no documentation that can show—'

'You certain of that, Mr Coleman?' Cooper asked, injecting innocence into his voice. 'Can I quote you on that?'

The aide seated beside Coleman tugged at his sleeve, rose, whispered something in his ear. Coleman nodded, frowned and then glared at Cooper. 'I've no desire to be quoted on any of these issues, Cooper. We are here today to give you a story—the reasons behind Iberica's attempt to take over control of Artaros. The reasons, and the strategy. I am not here to listen to wild mud-slinging—'

'I've made no statements, Mr Coleman,' Cooper said mildly. 'I've just asked questions. About matters of record. In the interests of the investors.'

'Loaded questions, which have no substance in reality,' Coleman insisted angrily. 'But let's take the gloves off here and get down to basics. I've said why I'm here. Why are *you* at this Press conference?'

'To get statements of the truth.'

'Or to serve the interests of the Artaros board?' Coleman asked swiftly. 'Not the shareholders, I stress, who might well be persuaded to sell their stock to me. And they'd do well to take that plunge. No, not in their interests, but the board, the weak, pusillanimous, negative group of men who are taking Artaros down a slippery slope.' Coleman straightened his slim frame indignantly. He glared around the group of journalists, then fixed his gaze on Cooper again.

'It's apparent to me that you don't come here in a genuine journalistic frame of mind to discover the reality behind the battle between Artaros and Iberica. You're nothing more than a front man, Cooper, and I recognize you as such. A front man for the Artaros board. The question—my question—is how much are they paying you to do their dirty work for them—what are you getting out of this performance you put on today?'

Cooper shrugged. 'I get no kick-back from Artaros. But I *do* like to get answers to questions. Like the question . . . is there any truth in the story that you're only launching through Switzerland into Europe because things are too hot for you in the States?'

As the room cleared slowly a couple of the journalists came up to Cooper and shook their heads. One gave him a light punch on the arm, and asked him what he knew that they didn't, but no attempt was made to persuade him to talk. There was a certain embarrassment among them as they left: Eric was left with the clear impression they all felt that Cooper's performance had been less than professional. There had been too much of the muck-raking element in it. Phil Cooper himself was in no hurry to leave, sitting there with a large whisky in front of him—courtesy of Matt Coleman and CI Iberica.

'I appreciate that,' Cooper said, smiling at the dark liquid in his glass.

'I'm sorry, Phil,' Eric said shortly.

'For what? Hey, come on, you fed me some stuff, I checked it out—that was my show, not yours. And if the other hacks think I went overboard, that's their problem. I knew what I was doing. But he's no pushover, our friend Coleman. The way he swung the story around against me personally . . . But he was wriggling all right, he was wriggling.'

'Are you telling me Bowles's information is sound?'

Cooper shrugged. 'As far as it goes. It wouldn't stand up in a courtroom, otherwise the US Government would have shoved Coleman behind bars. But it leaves me with a gut feeling . . . and I always trust my belly. Coleman is running from trouble in the States, and he thinks he's slipped their leash, left too few tracks to be caught. Bowles has given us ammunition, and I've fired the rounds for you. But it's for me, too. It's some time since I broke a really big story.'

'And this could be it?' Eric asked.

'I have that feeling,' Cooper replied with a half-controlled exultation.

'It could be the whisky.'

'That's veins, not head . . . and my head is buzzing,' Cooper said, and downed the drink.

They rose and walked to the door. They were on the fourth floor and as they waited for the lift a door opened to their left. Eric glanced across: it was the fresh-faced aide. He stepped back with a quick word, and the next moment Matt Coleman walked out of the room. He made his way directly towards them in a slow, measured stride that was somehow menacing in its control. He stopped in front of them, looking up with a frank curiosity at Phil Cooper towering over him.'That was quite a performance, Mr Cooper. I enjoyed it.'

'You didn't seem to.'

Coleman smiled thinly. He gave Eric the impression of a coiled snake, waiting patiently to strike. 'Appearances can be deceptive. Yours, for instance.' He let his cold eyes dwell on Cooper's untidy appearance. 'No, I enjoyed the performance for what it was worth. Hot air. Bluster. The dredging up of old tales. Of course, it led to an . . . over-reaction on my part. I called your motives into question. But financial journalists do not, of course, have corrupt relationships with big companies. Or not often anyway.' His glance slipped to Eric. 'You haven't introduced us, Mr Cooper.'

'My name's Ward.'

'Also a journalist?'

'No.' Eric hesitated. 'A lawyer.'

'Making sure Cooper stays within the bounds of the law? You should have given him better advice.'

'Mr Cooper's not my client.'

'Ah. And what's your interest in this Press conference, Mr Ward?'

Eric stared at him directly. 'I'm a director of Martin and Channing.'

For a few seconds Matt Coleman's eyes were vague and uninterested. Then a change came over them, a glint of steel in their depths. He smiled coldly. 'Ah. I see. Martin and Channing. My enemy's friend.' He looked briefly up at Phil Cooper. 'Now I begin to understand. Martin and Channing.'

He turned, began to walk back towards the doorway where the aide waited. Then he paused, looking back. 'I've no idea at this stage, Mr Ward, where you got your tittle-tattle from, the stuff you clearly passed to Cooper—but I can make an educated guess. You should be aware that your informant is a bitter man, and a foolish one. He allows his judgement to be affected by emotion. I do not. And he is inclined . . . to tilt at windmills he cannot possibly damage. Don't take a leaf out of his book, Mr Ward.' He smiled. 'You could be so easily unhorsed. And that . . . it could be a painful experience.'

The underlying tone of menace left Eric with no illusions. It was designed to make clear to him that Matt Coleman could deal ruthlessly with those who might stand in his way.

Eric and Phil Cooper said nothing as they made their way down in the lift. At the doors of the Hilton they stood side by side, squinting out into the sunshine.

'Tough guy,' Eric said.

'Talks tough.'

'Will you be going on with it?'

'Far as I can,' Cooper grunted. 'I've got to make some calls to the States, might turn something up. But why did you admit to him that you were tied in with Martin and Channing?'

Eric shrugged. The whole business left an unpleasant taste in his mouth. Greg Bowles's defence to the Iberica attack was too personal—even if he had to admit that the questioning had shaken Coleman more than he had expected. 'I just felt . . . well, why should I hide behind the draperies? He's bound to find out sooner or later, as the defence continues.'

'You've too much conscience, lad. Finance is a dirty business. It's all about money, you see.' He half-turned, about to leave. 'I'll get back to the office. File the story.'

'You'll use the stuff today?'

'Hell no! Not directly, anyway. Just put out some warning shots. I'll need something harder—but I was encouraged by Coleman's reaction. He's not scared, he's angry. And that's almost as good as scared.'

Eric nodded. 'There's something else. Something not in the file. I can't put my finger on it exactly, but I believe that Coleman was involved in a company called North Lagoon, Inc. I understand he used it in some way to fund some of his operations in the States. Do you know anything about the company?'

Cooper shook his head. 'Rings no bells. Want me to check?'

'It might be interesting. And talking of lagoons, do you know anything about a shipbroking firm called International Charters?'

Cooper's face broke into a broad smile. 'Certainly do.' He shook his head and chuckled. 'What *is* it about you? You get your nose into more mucky deals than anyone I've ever come across.'

'International Charters?'

'That's right. They're in trouble.'

'So what's the problem there?'

'Their files got called in. Fraud Squad.' Cooper looked carefully at Eric. 'This anything to do with the Iberica bid?'

Eric shook his head. 'No. Something else again. But if you know the principal of the company—'

'Les Reynolds.'

'Can you get me an introduction?'

'Nothing easier, my son. By way of the usual arrangement?'

Eric hesitated. 'I shouldn't think there's any story in it for you.'

'But if there is, I get first crack at it?'

Eric smiled. 'I'm sure that can be arranged.'

'Fine. In that case, I'll do the necessary. I'll be in touch in a couple of days. See you.'

He got into the first cab available and left. Eric thought of taking a taxi himself, but then decided to walk under the subway and stroll in Hyde Park for a while.

He did not stay long. He felt cold. It could have had something to do with the memory of the tone in which Matt Coleman had spoken to him.

To go against the Coleman windmill could be a painful experience. Eric had no doubt Coleman was talking of broken bones.

3

Jackie Parton sat easily in the chair in Eric's office on the Quayside and accepted the whisky that Eric offered him: he had always been partial to a good whisky. He occasionally drank to excess when he was with friends in the local pubs and clubs on Tyneside, but the result was the emergence of a certain maudlin streak, Eric had heard, and an inclination to sing. His rendition of *The Waters of Tyne* was not noted for its tunefulness but on the other hand he was not the sort on whom the police called out the dogs on a Saturday night in Grey Street.

He had been a successful and popular jockey who had ridden a great deal at Newcastle Races and had attracted a strong and vociferous local following. Injury, the northern betting rings, a suspicion of bribery and a bad beating from some touts had brought a premature end to his career, but he was well liked and trusted on Tyneside, and Eric used him from time to time because of his local knowledge.

'Not got much for you this time, Mr Ward,' Jackie Parton said, sipping his whisky with an appreciative air.

'Just what have you found out?'

Parton fingered his scarred nose thoughtfully. 'Well, you're right enough that Harry Staughton was a Sunderland lad. There's still a few around Roker way remember him—contemporaries, like. One says he remembers him well as a kid because he had a great appetite—as he put it, Harry could put away more taties than a pig. But he's been away from the scene a long time, they tell me. Good fifteen years and more, they say.'

'What was his background?'

'Canny enough. His old man worked in the shipyards—supervisor, like, made a good wage, sent young Harry to grammar school in Wallsend. But talk is he got a bit big for his boots, you knaa. Looked down on the old folk, like. Got out quick once he got the chance, moved away from Sunderland.'

'Did he do any business on Tyneside?'

'Seems like, Mr Ward. Started out working for a car dealer up at Pelton Fell of all places. I mean, the Fell . . . But then he got took in by one of the building societies as a clerk, switched to a broking firm, got fed up with that and lit out. Since then, not a lot's been heard of him.'

'He went overseas.'

'Aye, so I'm told. Oh yeah, there was also some business he got tied in with up at Alnmouth. Chandlers; shipping business. But he wasn't there long.'

Eric frowned. 'Any talk about the kind of man he was?'

'Smooth operator. Even as a youngster he could charm the birds. Used to hang out down at the old Pavilion Saturday nights. Same sort of charm came through in his business. Moved jobs fast enough, but he was always talked of as bright, pushy, and sort of ambitious. In a hurry, like.'

'To go where?'

'He didn't seem to know. But . . .' Jackie Parton wrinkled his pulped features thoughtfully. 'You knaa, Mr

Ward, there's something about him that sort of smells. People I spoke to, they said he was arl reet, but it was what they weren't sayin' that I was listening to.'

'I don't understand.'

'They was saying something else with their eyes.'

'Such as?'

'They didn't want to see him again.'

Eric raised his eyebrows. He stared at the ex-jockey thoughtfully. 'Now why would that be?'

Jackie Parton smiled. 'I don't know, sir. But lemme put it like this to you. There's some fellers you get on with real well, you knaa? You enjoy their company. But you don't want to see them again because it embarrasses you.'

'Why?'

'Because you feel they didn't spend time with you because they liked you. No, they was using you, like, and later you got to realize it. Nothing to put your finger on, maybe, but . . . well, if you've been used, you don't want to knaa, do yer?'

'He was a con man?'

'Nobody said that. But no one mentioned the word trust, either.'

'I see. And you learned nothing about where he might be now?'

'Not a sniff. I'll keep asking around, Mr Ward, but I got a feeling about this one. I mean, most people you can get a picture of. Not this one. He could change to suit his company, like a . . . a . . .'

'Chameleon.'

'Thass right. What you said. He could stand out, but when he'd gone, people couldn't sort of remember much about him. Except he was charming, good company, and all that. I know you gave me that photograph of him, but that's not what I'm talking about. Photographs sometimes don't tell you much. You got to deal with a man face to face to recognize him. Know what I mean?' The ex-jockey paused reflectively. 'No, I got a feeling this is going to be a tough one, Mr Ward. This Staughton guy, he's hollow. If he's swanned it, my guess is he's away with enough to live on, and with a new identity. It's just a feeling, mind, but I've known villains . . . No one's given me to believe Harry Staughton was a villain, not as such, but let's just say I don't believe he was whistle-clean. No, not by a long stirrup . . .'

Eric had hoped Jackie Parton would have been able to come up with something more positive. He himself made some discreet inquiries among old friends in the police, and with a couple of less reputable contacts than Jackie Parton, men he had used to tap the underworld networks in the past but he drew a blank. Staughton had no criminal record, and he hadn't got into any sort of trouble, it seemed, while he had lived in the North-East. Nor were they aware that he might have returned. He was certainly not on the electoral rolls on Tyneside.

Nor did Reuben Podmore have anything to offer. The Investment Manager of Stanley Investments was an old acquaintance, who was now in business linked with Martin and Channing and Eric trusted him: he also respected the old man's knowledge of the financial world in the North-East. But although Podmore had vaguely heard of Harry Staughton, it was in only some minor financial capacity, and although he asked around for Eric, among his own contacts on Tyneside and Teesside, he had nothing to offer. Harry Staughton had made no great impression among the financial institutions in the north, and there were no traces to follow now.

Simon Chan's belief that Eric's local networks would bring results was looking thin. It made that much more important Eric's meeting with Les Reynolds: the managing director of International Charters had certainly had recent dealings with the man Simon Chan wanted to find.

Phil Cooper had been true to his word. He had contacted Reynolds and arranged an interview. Eric took the train down from Newcastle to Plymouth and stayed at an hotel on the Hoe before going to Reynolds's office at ten in the morning.

It was only a short walk from the hotel. It was pleasant enough, strolling across the greensward of the Hoe where traditionally Drake had played his game of bowls, past the seventeenth-century Citadel commanding the height above Sutton Pool and the Cattewater. In its day it had been an example of the most modern fortress design: now it brooded impotently over the tourist industry that thronged during the summer months into the Barbican, its ancient armaments trained blindly seawards.

The yacht harbour was busy; the hulls of the boats moored there were close packed and as Eric walked along the harbourfront towards the narrow, twisting streets of the Barbican, largely renovated now to form tourist shops and restaurants, he felt a certain surprise that Les Reynolds should have made his base here. It seemed a long way from Singapore.

Reynolds met him at the top of the stairs. The office front was modest enough, set back behind the main street, but the furnishings were impressive, and the girl at reception was polite and attractive. Reynolds's office was a long, narrow room which overlooked the harbour itself, and the hills beyond, sweeping up towards the inland moors. He shook hands with Eric, arranged for some coffee to be sent up and smiled.

It was an attractive smile, and Eric warmed to him immediately. Reynolds was just above middle height, with close-cropped curly hair of a sandy colour. He had a schoolboy's face: a small, smiling mouth and bubbling, enthusiastic voice. His eyes were quick, cheerful and dancing with mischief. He clearly spent much of his time out of doors, for his cheeks were weathered and tanned, and his handclasp was firm, his skin roughened, Eric guessed, from sailing activities. He was dressed in slacks, an open-necked shirt and a dark blue sweater with a Gucci motif on the left shoulder. He was heavily built, and fit, though in middle age he might develop a paunch. He was in his late thirties, and sunny of temperament.

'So you know Phil Cooper?' he asked.

'We've done business from time to time,' Eric replied.

'Phil and I go way back,' Reynolds said, grinning. 'I remember the little bugger at school. He and I got some tannings, I can tell you! All harmless stuff, of course, but the headmaster didn't see it that way. Felt he had to instil some responsibility into us. Didn't really work, though, you know!'

'You've kept in touch over the years?'

Reynolds shook his head. 'Not really. He went his way, I went mine. Our paths crossed again recently, really. It was a surprise to me to find he'd gone into financial journalism—I mean, the bugger couldn't spell at school! But when the Inland Revenue landed on my back—you'll have heard about that?'

Eric hesitated. 'I . . . Phil said you were having certain problems.'

'You can say that again!' There was a tap on the door and the girl from downstairs brought in coffee for them. Reynolds thanked her, and watched her leave. 'Cracker, don't you think? Polperro maid, really, come to the big city. A certain simplicity of soul . . . Anyway, what was I saying?'

'You were talking about Cooper.'

'Oh, yeah, that's right. Fact is, when the IR came down on me and the company got into trouble, it was Phil who turned up on the doorstep with questions about my financial status. I mean, can you believe it? We got drunk, instead.'

'He came down here to Plymouth?'

Reynolds shook his head. 'No, no, the London office. This isn't my main pad: it suits me to keep a Plymouth base because we do a fair bit of chartering down here, and it also gets me away for the odd week or so out of the Smoke.

I can get a bit of decent sailing in here. It just so happened when Phil rang me to suggest we met, I was down here.'

'I did wonder . . . International Charters . . .'

'What's in a name, hey?' Reynolds sipped his coffee. 'Fact is, we're not a large organization. Commission work, basically. Oh, we turn over a fair business. The London office pulls most of the heavy stuff—Indian Ocean, Pacific, that sort of thing. Down here, it's backwater deals—but it's not a bad place to work from time to time.' He grinned affably. 'Anyway, what can I do to help you?'

'I'm making some inquiries on behalf of a client.'

'Ahuh.'

'I understand you negotiated a chartering contract some time ago, between Artaros SA and Malaysia Mobile.'

Les Reynolds frowned thoughtfully. He sipped his coffee, then rose and strolled across to the window. His fingers played with the motif on the left breast of his sweater. 'Ah yes. The *Arctic Queen*.' He paused. 'What do you want to know about it?'

'According to Greg Bowles, the deal was struck with the Charter Manager of Malaysia Mobile through your agency.'

'That about sums it up.'

'So you know Harry Staughton?'

'Know him?' Les Reynolds laughed, but some of the warmth had gone from his voice. 'Oh yes, Harry and I did some business together.'

'Successfully.'

'At first.'

Carefully Eric said, 'I've been told the *Arctic Queen* wasn't one of Malaysia Mobile's best buys.'

Reynolds snorted happily. 'That's true enough. Luckily, I was just the broker. I got the commission, whatever happened to the ship. But . . .' He hesitated, eyeing Eric with a frown. 'You're a lawyer, I understand.'

'That's right.'

'You're working for Malaysia Mobile. That means for Simon Chan.'

'I am. Do you know him?'

Reynolds shook his head. 'No, I never met him. When I was out in Singapore, my dealings were with Harry as Charter Manager for the company. But Chan . . . he's not pursuing the *Arctic Queen* business, is he? It's yesterday's news. I mean, you're not acting on that affair?'

'Not really. But I'd like to hear about the *Arctic Queen*, since Staughton was involved. It was a time charter, wasn't it?'

'Ahuh. With an option to purchase. Harry exercised the option, and I did that deal for him too.'

'What happened to the *Arctic Queen* thereafter?'

Reynolds eyed Eric for a moment, then grinned wickedly. 'Oh, she's still afloat, believe me. But she was always something of a rustbucket, you know. Still, it's up to the buyer.'

'*Caveat emptor*,' Eric supplied drily.

'Not up to the seller to point out defects. Nor the commission agent either! No, but the fact is, Harry didn't hold on to the old *Arctic Queen* too long. I was able to set him up with another deal.'

'To sell on?'

Reynolds shrugged. 'I made the contact with Ocean Distribution once he'd pointed me in their direction. I negotiated a deal whereby the Ocean people bought the *Arctic Queen* from Malaysia Mobile—but then chartered it back to MM on a three-year charter. I gather . . . well, I'd have to refresh my memory, but my files have been bloody well impounded at the moment by the Fraud Squad—I mean, can you believe it! Anyway, I was saying, I gather there's a dispute between Ocean Distribution and Malaysia Mobile over the charter.'

'What's it about?'

Reynolds walked back to the desk and sat down, draping one leg over the arm of the chair, easily. He shrugged, waved his coffee mug. 'You'd better ask Simon Chan about that. It's his neck. But all this . . . why are you coming to me? Chan can give you chapter and verse about the *Arctic Queen* deal: he had a seat in the choir stalls.'

'I'm just interested in Harry Staughton's part in it. Helps to give me a picture of the man. I'm trying to trace him.'

'The best of luck,' Reynolds said quietly.

'So you don't know where he is?'

'No. I've no idea.' Reynolds swung his leg down, and straightened in his seat, staring at Eric. 'Why are you looking for him?'

'I'm just interested in finding out where he is at the moment,' Eric replied evasively.

'You won't find it easy.'

'Why?'

'Because he's flown the coop.'

'How do you know that?'

Reynolds set down his mug in a heavy, deliberate movement. His cheerfulness had dissipated. His eyebrows came together in a frown. 'I liked Harry. We did business, we hit some of the night spots in KL and Singapore, he was good company. We got on well. And I trusted him.' He laughed suddenly. 'He had what the Yanks call charaysma—you know? I trusted him. It was a mistake.'

'In what way?' Eric asked.

Reynolds avoided the question. 'Why does Chan want you to find Harry Staughton?'

Eric hesitated. 'It's a confidential matter. I can't explain to you what my client—'

'Hah! I don't think you need to!' Reynolds shook his head dismissively. 'My guess is Chan will be in a similar boat to me. Harry conned me—it's highly likely I won't be the only one around in that position. But I gave up on it. Chan clearly hasn't.'

'Gave up on what?'

Les Reynolds leaned back in his chair, right hand across his chest, stroking the motif on his left shoulder thoughtfully. 'No reason why I shouldn't tell you, I suppose . . .

You see, when I negotiated the sale between Artaros and Malaysia Mobile, Harry and I struck up a sort of friendship. We got on well, we sort of talked of the possibility of business ventures together. A little later, he came to me and asked me to handle the Ocean Distribution deal. I was happy enough: it would be a good commission, and to be honest, I could see his point in getting rid of the *Arctic Queen*, because, well, the scene was changing on the chartering front and in a few years she'd be heading for the breaker's yard anyway. But then he came back to me. He wanted included in the contract a three-year charter back: Malaysia Mobile were keen to sell, but still needed the *Queen* for a period.'

'Did that surprise you, in view of the fact that there were doubts about the *Arctic Queen*'s seaworthiness?'

Reynolds's eyes widened. 'Hold on . . . that's overstating things a bit. She was OK for a charter of that period. It's just her long-term future . . . Anyway, never mind, that's not the point.'

'You negotiated the charter back to Malaysia Mobile.'

'That's right. And that meant I was picking up a hefty commission. But I never did.'

'How do you mean?'

'I never got the commission. My friend Harry Staughton did a runner. I've seen neither hide nor hair of him since. And I got to say, that doesn't please the hell out of me, I can tell you!'

'Did you try to trace him?'

'Are you kidding?' Reynolds snorted again. 'At that time, I'd have broken his back if I could have got my hands on him! But I tell you, he just faded. Disappeared. I suspect he holed up somewhere in Europe, that's my guess, but I've never heard a damn thing about him once he skedaddled. Then I cooled. Other things began to preoccupy me. Like the bloody Fraud Squad.' He growled, deep in his throat. 'I'm clear, you know that? They phoned me yesterday. They'll be returning my files. No action to be taken. But what about my business reputation in the meanwhile? I ought to sue.'

'You have someone to take action against?'

"Do you mean do I know who tried to put the finger on me? Oh, I know who that is, believe me, Mr Ward! And maybe I'll do something about that.' He was silent for a little while. 'As for Harry, well, I've written it off. A lot of money . . . but I liked him, and, what the hell. Put it down to experience. The bastard!'

Eric hesitated. 'If you do come across any trail, I'd be grateful to hear about it.'

Les Reynolds nodded. He finished his coffee, and held Eric's glance. 'OK, we'll do a trade.'

'What sort of trade?'

'You're a lawyer, right? And you're acting for Simon Chan, turning over stones, trying to find me old mucker Harry. Well, the deal is this. Anything I find out, I'll let you have. I can't promise you anything, and I certainly won't be active, but I suppose you never know—something might turn up. Harry might even have the nerve to get in touch with me!'

'That's fair enough.'

'That's only my part of it, my friend. The rest . . . well, let's keep in touch. I respect Phil Cooper and he speaks highly of you. And if I decide to take action against the bastards who set me up with the Fraud Squad, I'll need some legal advice.'

'I'm not sure . . .'

'I'd appreciate you acting for me, if I decide to take action.'

'I'd have to know more about it,' Eric replied carefully.

'Goes without saying,' Reynolds said, beaming. He stuck out a large hand, took Eric's and pumped it heartily. 'Let's leave it like that. We'll go our separate directions and keep in touch about Harry Staughton. After all, both Chan and I stand to benefit, don't we? And as to the other thing—

once I decide, I'll get hold of you and give you some business. Can't say fairer than that now, can we?'

Outside, the gulls were wheeling raucously above the masted harbour.

CHAPTER 3

1

The rain came slanting down, driven by a north-easterly that brought in scudding dark clouds from the coast, cloaking the Cheviot in a thick mist and lowering the temperature by several degrees. Though Sedleigh Hall was centrally heated—Lord Morcomb had not believed in shivering in mediæval splendour—a fire had been laid in the open fireplace of the drawing-room as a courtesy to the guests, so they could relax in front of a cheerful blaze after the meeting that Anne had arranged at the Hall was over.

It had been a full meeting of the board. The first day had been devoted to Morcomb Enterprises business *per se*; the second day Simon Chan had been invited to attend to meet the full board and open preliminary discussions, with an informal agenda, about possible cooperative ventures between the company and Malaysia Mobile.

Eric had not been present, of course—he held no status on the board and had long resisted Anne's attempts to employ him. He had promised to get back in time for the evening of Chan's visit, however, so as soon as he had finished in court with the firearms case he'd been involved with, he made his way back to the Quayside, cleared his desk and drove north.

It had not been a good journey: the wind buffeted him on the open stretches of the A1, and the driving rain made the road treacherous. The necessity to concentrate hard and peer through the smeared windscreen brought the old, familiar needle-points of pain back to his eyes, and it was with a sense of relief that he finally swung into the crunching driveway of Sedleigh Hall.

He had showered, changed and was in the bedroom, all but ready to go down, by the time Anne came in, exhausted after the long meeting with the board and Simon Chan.

'Hello, darling. Glad you made it,' she said and reached for him.

After he had kissed her, Eric asked, 'Had a good day?'

She grimaced. 'Simon Chan is as inscrutable as I've heard all Chinese are. We haven't had a bloody thing from him.'

'No commitments?'

'None whatsoever. Oh, he's extremely polite,' she said with a grimace as she kicked off her shoes, 'interested in all we do and have to offer, makes all the right noises, goes into long, convoluted expressions of regard for Morcomb Enterprises, but when I look at my notes at the end of the day there's . . . nothing.'

Eric laughed and helped her unzip her dress. 'Maybe he'll loosen up over the brandy.'

'I damn well hope so. Anyway, Eric, be a dear and go down ahead of me. They'll all be changing for dinner and it'll take them a little time, but you know how it is. There are one or two there who'll develop a raging thirst long before I'm ready to join them. I'll have to shower and make myself beautiful—'

'More beautiful.'

'*Evening* kind beautiful, then.' She grinned. 'So will you look after them until I make my entrance?'

'Flow down the stairs, my love, and I'll make sure they notice.'

She gave him a hug and retreated to the bathroom. Eric went down to the drawing-room. Dinner was not scheduled for another hour, but he had no doubt Sir Toby Fletcher would soon be in for his gin and tonic, and the desiccated accountant Hartnell, who was financial adviser to the board, would want his dry sherry. Two of the board members had already left, he understood, with other engagements, but there were still six of them to entertain. He got a whisky and soda for himself while he waited, one foot on Lord Morcomb's old cast-iron fireguard. He sipped the drink slowly, aware of the dull ache behind his eyes but reluctant to acknowledge it. He was hardly aware of anyone entering the room until he heard the waiter asking what drink was desired.

Eric turned. It was Charles Davison. He had been at the board meeting in his capacity as legal adviser. He strolled forward, strikingly handsome in his dinner jacket and aware of it, and extended his hand to Eric. Eric was forced to take it. The handshake was like Davison: forceful, confident and competitive.

'You got back in time then, Eric.'

'Just about.'

'I imagine Anne will have told you we've had a difficult day. Couldn't get that wily old Chinaman to move at all. Are they all so difficult, I wonder? How did you manage in Singapore?'

'I wasn't dealing with the Chinese,' Eric replied, unreasonably annoyed that Davison knew he had been to Singapore. There was no reason why Anne shouldn't have told the man, innocently enough.

'Chinese-owned company, though, I understand—Artaros SA. I hear you're undertaking the defence for them against Iberica. Strong stuff. Saw a piece about it all, by that Cooper chap. Coleman sounds a shady character.'

'There are a few around,' Eric said drily.

'Now I wonder who you mean?' Davison eyed him with a sly grin. 'Do you get on any easier with Simon Chan than we seem to?'

Eric shrugged, non-committally. When he made no reply, Davison waited until his drink had arrived and then smiled at Eric. 'Cheers, then. What sort of day have you had? In court, I understand.'

'Nothing in your league.'

'Tut, tut, it's all in support of blind Justice, surely! You had a case on?'

'Firearms.'

'What was the issue?'

'Whether semi-automatic pistols are within the list of prohibited weapons under the Firearms Act 1988.'

'They are, surely!'

Eric shrugged. 'There's a doubt.'

'What the hell was your client doing with such a weapon, anyway?'

'He's a farmer. He uses it to cull large vermin—rats, mainly.'

'A semi-automatic?'

Wearily Eric said, 'He was ill-advised. The Act prohibits self-loading and pump-action rifles. The man's been using them for years. Now he's had to get rid of them, he thought a semi-automatic would do the trick.'

'It will . . . for getting large vermin. But how large, hey? And what species?' Davison eyed Eric maliciously. 'Are you sure that's what he wanted it for? No wife trouble, for instance? No question of midnight hold-ups on the Great North Road? I say, really, Eric, the kind of clientele you handle down in your Quayside practice, I wonder that you can sleep soundly at nights. You ought to move up into the city, my friend, deal with people who are . . . respectable.'

Eric returned the glance steadily. 'Let's not talk too noisily about respectable clients, Davison.'

'Or respectable lawyers?' Davison grinned unpleasantly and turned away. 'Ah, Sir Toby, you've arrived. I think I'm correct when I say yours is a gin and tonic, is it not?'

Davison was always attentive to the titled, even in dispensing other people's hospitality. It was the way he had expanded his practice, Eric thought sourly to himself.

*

Dinner passed off uneventfully. Anne came down in an off-the-shoulder evening dress that was perhaps a shade too formal for an occasion of this kind but none of the men present were inclined to complain. At the far end of the table Eric was able to take a detached view of the way the board members looked at her, and the manner in which Charles Davison, in particular, attempted to monopolize the conversation with her. Simon Chan was discretion itself; quiet, reserved and extremely polite.

Sir Toby, sitting on Eric's right, tried to pump him on the Iberica bid, for Cooper's article had caused quite a stir and it was common knowledge that Martin and Channing were involved in the Artaros defence. Eric played him off easily enough, largely because he had nothing he could add to what had appeared in Cooper's article. There had been a resounding silence from Singapore, although Greg Bowles was expected to arrive in England early the next week for a conference.

'The share prices are continuing to rise, anyway,' Sir Toby said, 'on the back of the speculation surrounding the Iberica bid. If Coleman is to complete his raid, it won't be too long before he gets out, in my opinion. What do you think, Eric?'

'It's quite possible.'

'Once a shark, always a shark. Whatever he said at that Press conference, he's not going to give up his arbitraging ways.'

'I'm sure Eric will be launching an appropriate defence,' Davison commented with a mocking smile. Sir Toby hardly heard. He was quickly launched on his assessments of the market. It left little room for other points of view.

When dinner was over the group returned to the drawing-room for coffee and brandy. The conversation became general, Davison sitting near Anne with Sir Toby hovering appreciatively. Eric played the host for a while but eventually caught Simon Chan's glance. Chan inclined his head slightly, and Eric made a gesture towards the doorway. Eric met him there. 'I think we could take a few minutes in the library, Mr Chan, without being too rude.'

'I am in your hands, Mr Ward.'

The library was a room Eric loved, and one in which he spent a great deal of his leisure time. It was a large room with a splendidly carved seventeenth-century oak table in the centre. The walls were lined with oak bookshelves and the range of books displayed demonstrated the somewhat idiosyncratic tastes of several generations of Morcombs. Leather bindings gleamed with gold; old law books shone with their red cloth and gilt lettering. Chan exclaimed in delight, and spent a few minutes wandering along the shelves, touching gently, inspecting.

'An interesting collection, Mr Ward.'

'Anne's father. And his before him.'

'The law books also?'

'They're mainly mine. Of historic interest, of course—those, and the legal biographies.'

'Of course. But it is a pleasure to step into a room with a past, and know it belongs to one who values the thoughts and delights of his ancestors. But—' he turned to look at Eric carefully, his narrow eyes thoughtful—'there is also the present to consider . . . and the future. Have you gained any success in your inquiries?'

'Harry Staughton left little or no mark in the North-East, Mr Chan. I've made use of the network you thought might be useful, but it's come up with nothing.'

'That is a disappointment. I hoped there might be some lead to his movements.'

'I'm afraid not. However, I have been following other lines of inquiry. In particular, I've been talking to people who have been in contact with him of recent years.'

'Such as?'

'The managing director of Artaros—Greg Bowles. And the man who arranged the charter and sale of the *Arctic Queen*—Les Rowlands. It seems you're not alone in your experiences of Harry Staughton, Mr Chan. There are others around who have no cause to love him.'

Chan said nothing for a moment. He prowled around the room, looking at the shelves, his black hair gleaming under the ceiling lights. 'They advise you Staughton is a man whose character is . . . unreliable?'

'That's about it.'

'But they have no information as to his whereabouts?'

'No. But both express an interest in knowing where he might be.' Eric hesitated. 'Mr Chan, I'm a little curious about that *Arctic Queen* deal. As I understand it, the ship had had a chequered history. Harry Staughton chartered the vessel from Artaros, but a man of his experience must have known that a purchase thereafter was risky.'

Chan perambulated onwards with his back to Eric. 'He told the board that we should purchase at the end of the twelve-month charter because the likelihood was that charter prices would rise.'

'But within a short period after that, Staughton approached Les Reynolds at Intenational Charters to arrange a sale of Ocean Distribution—with a charter back to Malaysia Mobile. It doesn't make sense, Mr Chan. Why sell what was going to be a liability, but at the same time charter back at a time when prices were still supposedly rising? It was like throwing away the opportunity to make money—giving the chance to Ocean Distribution, not to Malaysia Mobile.'

Chan turned, to stare at Eric. 'It was a question that was asked at my board.'

'Of Staughton?'

'He was not available.'

'But this was some time ago. Staughton was still working for you—'

'You do not understand, I think. These matters did not come to light immediately. As Vice President and Charter Manager of Malaysia Mobile, Mr Staughton had a considerable freedom of activity. He had certain clear functions, and he was not interfered with. When the matters *did* come to light, he was summoned to appear before the board. That was when he disappeared. And subsequent investigations disclosed the problem that I explained to you. The reason why I need to interview Mr Staughton.'

Eric was puzzled. 'But wouldn't this have come out in end of year accounts? I mean, how long was it before your people became aware of the *Arctic Queen* transactions?'

Simon Chan paused. He folded his arms and watched Eric for a few moments thoughtfully. Then he shrugged. 'I do not see why you should be so interested in this matter.'

'It could help me understand Staughton. And it could lead me to other contacts, who might be able to help.'

Chan grimaced. 'I think it is hardly possible. But . . . the facts did not come to light before the board of Malaysia Mobile until we decided to relinquish the charter of the *Arctic Queen.* Rates were rising fast; we did not need the vessel, certainly not at the rate of £350,000 a month. It was then that we entered into a dispute with the new owners—Ocean Distribution.'

'They wanted to hold you to the charter?'

'Exactly.' Chan's face was impassive. 'But we did not agree on the terms of the charter.'

'Weren't they clear?'

'The documentation we received was clear. But it did not . . . match the documentation held by Ocean Distribution.'

'I don't understand.'

Chan shrugged. 'There are several issues. They hinge on one fact. Mr Staughton had no authority to sign the charter in the terms he did. But in addition, those terms are themselves a matter for dispute. The background also . . .'

'What's the status of the dispute at the moment?'

'We are in litigation,' Chan said drily. 'For us, it is a clear issue. Staughton had no authority to enter the agreement. But all this is a sideshow.'

'I'm not so sure—'

'The director of Ocean Distribution is called Paul Lintern. He is an angry man. He would give you a different story, I am sure. But my business does not demand that you pursue this line of inquiry. The essential thing is that I find Mr Staughton soon, before my board meets. And you do not seem to be making much progress.' Chan paused, sighing. 'However, perhaps I should let you follow your own roads. You have a reputation, Mr Ward, in the City. It is one that suggests you have a . . . nose for finding out things.' He held Eric's glance steadily. 'Find this out for me, and quickly. Find Harry Staughton. And I don't care how you do it!'

Eric nodded. It was now his turn to hold Simon Chan's glance. 'If that's the case, I think I would like to pursue the matter of the *Arctic Queen*. You'd have no objection if I made contact with this man Lintern?'

Chan drew his lips back over his teeth in an uncomfortable grimace. 'An approach . . . you would need to be careful, Mr Ward. I have said, Ocean Distribution and Malaysia Mobile are in the throes of litigation. We would not want that position we take to be . . . ah . . . compromised.'

'I can assure you, all I'd want from Lintern is some background on his dealings with Staughton. I didn't get a great deal from Les Reynolds about the affair—he was inclined to say it was all really down to Staughton, and he himself just acted as a go-between.'

Simon Chan shrugged. 'If your approach to Lintern will be along those lines, I foresee no problems for Malaysia Mobile. Indeed, it might, on second thoughts, be to our advantage. You might be able to discover just what line Ocean Distribution will be taking.'

'You already have depositions, I imagine.'

'That's so. We seem to be in direct conflict. It is almost as though we are not talking about the same documentation. We hold a simple one-year charter back after sale. It would seem Mr Lintern has something quite different. But if you do talk to Lintern, who knows? There may be something you can discover which will be to the advantage of Malaysia Mobile. The company,' he added after a moment,' would be grateful.'

Eric nodded, but made no response. He stepped aside, and began to lead the way back out of the library to return to the drawing-room where the others had gathered.

As they approached the open door Simon Chan touched him lightly on the arm. 'I know you will do all in your power to help our cause. Lintern may assist you . . . or he may not. Do remember, nevertheless, Mr Ward, what your primary objective is. Find Harry Staughton!'

2

Greg Bowles flew in a few days later.

A meeting was arranged at Martin and Channing's offices, but although Leonard Channing put in an appearance to welcome Bowles to the board room, he soon excused himself after taking a quick cup of coffee with them. It was clear he intended keeping himself well out of harm's way as far as the tactics to defend Artaros were concerned.

Bowles had brought a small entourage of dark-suited, earnest young men with him. He, and they, expressed themselves satisfied with the opening shots of the campaign, as they had appeared in Phil Cooper's article.

'But there's more that you could be doing,' Bowles insisted to Eric. 'We've dug up some further facts about Coleman's involvement with the Securities and Exchange Commission way back in 'eighty-seven. Coleman apparently filed information with the SEC which was untrue.'

The sallow young man at his elbow nodded vehemently. 'He failed to disclose an agreement with shareholders of Lawson Properties, a company he was trying to get control of. He didn't respond to the SEC charges—he just changed the information submitted to them. Later, when Coleman tried to block a management buyout in the company a New York judge threw it out of court. The judge referred to the earlier SEC problem and said, I quote, "Coleman came to court seeking equity with unclean hands."'

'I want that leaked in the British papers,' Bowles muttered.

'Is it in the public domain?' Eric asked.

'It never got much coverage at the time. Coleman had some pull with a number of politicians who saw to it the news never went big,' Bowles said sourly.

'There's another line of inquiry you might follow up,' Eric suggested.

'Yes?'

Bowles's eagerness was obvious. Eric hesitated. He had only that morning received the answer to the question he had put to Phil Cooper. He was still not happy about the nature of the campaign against Iberica's bid: it smacked too much of dirty tricks for his peace of mind. Nevertheless, since he was acting for Artaros, he was bound to follow such leads. 'It relates to a company called North Lagoon, Inc.'

The sallow young man leaned back in his chair and glanced at Bowles. 'What about it?' he asked.

'I'd come across the name in some capacity or another, but I couldn't quite remember,' Eric replied. 'I asked a friend of mine to check.'

'And?'

'It's a pension fund company.'

'So?' Bowles snapped.

'Better check it out. If it's a company which Coleman controls—and I don't know that he does—and if he's been using it to fund corporate raids, which I suspect he has—'

'He could be in breach of SEC regulations and US law,' the sallow young man interposed.

Eric nodded. 'I'm in no position to check myself, but you'll need to look at shadow shareholders, cross-holdings between the North Lagoon company and others under the control of Coleman, and whether Coleman's Iberica operation itself has any relationship with North Lagoon.'

The sallow young man was scribbling furiously. 'I'll check it out straight away, Mr Bowles . . .'

They continued discussing strategies until lunch-time, when Bowles declared himself satisfied with the way things were going, and told his entourage they could make their way out: he would follow them in a moment. He remained behind, staring thoughtfully at Eric. 'You're running this show, Ward.'

'How do you mean?'

'Leonard Channing's ducked out. What is it—too mucky for him?'

Eric shrugged non-committally. 'I'll be reporting to him and the board in due course.'

'If it goes well, I imagine Channing will make the report. And if it doesn't . . . I guess you'll be making the statement,' Bowles said sarcastically. 'But that's your business. This North Lagoon thing—and the way you've handled the Press leak—I like the way you operate, Ward.'

'On this matter, I'm not sure I do.'

Bowles grinned. 'That's direct enough. Still, maybe we ought to talk sometime, about what you could do for Artaros, after all this is over.'

Eric was disinclined to tell him the thought of working for Bowles did not excite him. Instead, he said, 'Let's get the Iberica thing over first.'

'Hmmm. Yeah, could be you're right. Even so . . .' Bowles hesitated, as though unwilling to break off the conversation.

Eric began to move towards the door. Bowles stopped him.

'How are you getting on with that other business you're involved in?'

Eric frowned. 'Which do you mean?'

Bowles was clearly unwilling to come straight out with it. He shrugged. 'The . . . the Malaysia Mobile business.'

Eric turned to stare at him. 'It's progressing.'

Bowles didn't want to ask, but the words came out almost

in spite of himself. He turned away, with a studied carelessness, but there was an uncontrolled edge to his tone. 'Have you turned up anything on Harry Staughton yet?'

Eric hesitated. 'I can't say I have. The man seems to have dropped out of sight completely.' Bowles sighed, a weary, unpleasant sound, a combination of bitterness and anger. 'No trace of him?'

'Not yet.'

Bowles swung again to face him. 'You think you're going to find Staughton?'

'I don't know,' Eric replied, surprised by the tension in the man. His surprise was communicated to Bowles. After a moment he made a deliberate attempt to relax, remove the bitterness from his eyes. He let his shoulders slump, and moved away towards the door. He appeared angry with himself, for letting his interest in the matter spill over so obviously.

Eric followed him thoughtfully. What puzzled him was why Greg Bowles should so obviously be dwelling on the disappearance of a man he'd got the better of in a business deal.

Eric walked up the steps of the Reform Club at precisely eight o'clock. He had phoned Ocean Distribution and asked if he could speak to Paul Lintern; he had expected it would be difficult to arrange a meeting. When he had explained to Lintern who he was and who he represented, he was surprised by the alacrity with which Lintern agreed to make an appointment—even to the extent, when Eric explained his time in London was limited, that he agreed they should meet for a drink in the Reform Club. They fixed a time that evening, before Lintern went on to a business function in South Africa House.

Much of the old elegance of the club remained: the echoing hall, the tall pillars and the statues and paintings of long-dead politicians, but the trestle-table from which drinks were dispensed seemed an incongruous modernity in the surroundings. Eric waited for a few minutes, then seated himself on a leather settee just inside the main doors until Lintern made himself known. A waiter came forward and asked him who he expected to meet, then withdrew. A few people drifted in, one approached him, expecting a business acquaintance, but it was a good ten minutes before a middle-aged, greying man in a dark overcoat came hurrying into the hall, looking to right and left. He approached the waiter, was directed towards Eric, and came walking across swiftly.

'Ward? Paul Lintern. I'm terribly sorry I'm late. The usual story. If you don't get out of the office when you can . . . What'll you have to drink? Brandy and soda? Fine. Just a moment.'

He went back to the table, divesting himself of his coat and asking a waiter to take it away for him. He came across with two drinks and sat down beside Eric. 'There we are. Sorry this is all a bit rushed, but I have a function to attend with the ambassador this evening.'

'It suits me. I'll get the late train back north.'

Lintern had long, saturnine features and a prominent hooked nose, which must have been broken at some time, since it was also somewhat lopsided. He tended to finger it self-consciously from time to time. His mouth was thin and suspicious and his dress was precise, the carnation in his buttonhole suggesting old world values which might be out of place in the business he was in, if not in the Reform Club or South Africa House.

He sipped his drink and stared at Eric with keen grey eyes. 'Well then, Ward. I understand you're a solicitor and work with Simon Chan of Malaysia Mobile. That's all I do know.'

'I don't work with him,' Eric corrected, 'but *for* him. That is, I've accepted an assignment from him.'

'So you're not a corporate lawyer?'

'No. I have a practice in Newcastle on Tyne—and an interest in a merchant bank in the City.'

'I see.' Lintern sniffed and wrinkled his nose, as though he felt he had been inveigled into this meeting under false pretences. 'But it is about the—ah—litigation that you wanted to see me. I thought . . .'

He did not say what he thought. Eric waited a moment. 'It's a matter connected with the purchase and sale of the *Arctic Queen*.'

'That is your assignment?'

'Not exactly.' When Lintern frowned, Eric hastened to add, 'The assignment is connected but isn't central to the litigation. Rather, it concerns Harry Staughton.'

Lintern's view of Harry Staughton was made obvious by the unpleasant grunt he uttered. He eyed Eric distastefully, his eyes cold as a winter sea. 'He's a man I wish I'd never met.'

'Do you know what's happened to him?'

'I only wish I did! The reality is, it's that man I would like to proceed against, although I would have to bring in his company as well, of course, in view of the sums of money involved. But Staughton would be a key witness, and if our lawyers could get him in the witness-box . . .'

He waved his glass angrily, slopping some of the liquid on the marble floor.

'You don't know where he is?'

'No. Do you?'

Eric shook his head. 'I'm trying to find him.'

'Aren't we all?' Lintern's mouth was twisted, like bent iron. 'The man took me in completely—a self-confident, imposing liar. He's cost Ocean Distribution a hell of a lot of money, and landed us with litigation we could well do without.'

'How did it happen?'

'You don't know the story?' Lintern glowered, considering. 'You're not a Malaysia Mobile lawyer . . . but you're looking for Staughton. Well, the facts are to be public record, anyway, so there's no harm in telling you. It all concerns the *Arctic Queen*.'

'Staughton negotiated a charter and sale to you, that much I know.'

'It wasn't quite that simple,' Lintern snapped angrily. 'A commission broker—International Charters—came to us and made the necessary introductions.'

'I know the principal—Les Reynolds.'

'Reynolds . . . yes.' Lintern's eyes were hooded for a moment as he sat thinking. Then he went on. 'Reynolds set up the meetings and the arrangements whereby Harry Staughton would enter an agreement with us as Vice President and Charter Manager of Malaysia Mobile, to sell us the *Arctic Queen*. It seemed to be coming at a good price. Though there were reasons for that.'

Eric could guess what they were. Lintern was no fool. He would have weighed up the value of the vessel, recognized its likely limited lifespan and would have taken a calculated risk—writing it off eventually as a tax loss.

'Of course, we weren't interested in a straight sale. It's obvious, isn't it? Why should we purchase an asset of doubtful value unless we were certain we could make some sort of short-term return out of her? So we told Staughton that we'd purchase, but only on condition he could arrange a guaranteed charter for us. He went away to think about it.'

'How long a charter were you thinking of?' Eric asked.

'That was the critical point.' Lintern's cold eyes gleamed. 'As far as we were concerned, the very minimum period of charter we could contemplate would be three years. Less than that, it simply wasn't worth while pursuing the matter. We knew the state of the vessel was such that we'd have to write it off, and while there'd be tax advantages in that, a guaranteed charter was necessary to show us a profit in the early years. Anyway, Staughton came back with an offer.'

'He met your terms, with a three-year charter?'

'That's right. But with a proviso. He said he'd taken the matter to the board of Malaysia Mobile and they had authorized him to conclude the sale, together with the charter over a three-year period. But there was a condition. I should have known then . . .'

'What was the condition?' Eric asked.

'Staughton told me that while the board was agreeable to charter the vessel back for three years, for internal reasons—not least their tax position in Malaysia, about which I knew damn nothing, of course—it was necessary that the charter be entered into as three consecutive one-year charters. It could make no difference to us, he argued. We'd get our three-year cover, but it would have to be through three separate contracts. He was prepared to sign all three immediately, of course. Staughton was a persuasive man . . . and naturally it suited us as well, because we insisted as one of our conditions that the purchase price we paid over to Staughton was also in tranches, with a deduction of the first year charter price from the first payment. The agreement was reached, a bank draft made out in accordance with Staughton's instructions, and the necessary purchase papers were made out. And that was that.'

'Until?'

'Until a year had gone by,' Lintern growled. 'On the due date we made contact with the Singapore office of Malaysia Mobile in accordance with our agreement. We then requested the completion of the second of the three charters that had been agreed to. There was a long silence. We pressed—for we are talking of a significant sum of money—and then we learned that Harry Staughton was no longer in the Singapore office. He had . . . disappeared.' Lintern paused, eyeing his glass angrily. 'It seemed a matter of little moment at the time. After all, Malaysia Mobile were committed by the signature of their Charter Manager.'

He was silent for a little while. 'What happened then?' Eric asked.

Lintern grunted and shifted uneasily in his seat. 'Simon Chan came to see me.'

'Personally?'

'That's right.' Lintern's grey eyes glared at Eric, flinty

lights seeming to glow in their depths. 'A smooth character, our Mr Chan, don't you agree? Very polite, very courteous, but very positive. Malaysia Mobile had no intention of honouring their contract. They requested payment of the whole amount for the *Arctic Queen*, and refused to honour the second and third of the three one-year charters that we had agreed with them, through Harry Staughton.'

'Did Simon Chan give you any explanation?'

'Of course. The easy one. The obvious one. The matter of the sale of the *Arctic Queen* had never been to the board of Malaysia Mobile.'

'But Staughton—'

'Had *said* he'd taken it to the board. But it had never happened. No, he'd arranged the sale on his own initiative. Moreover, Chan wanted the total price of the purchase from us—even though we'd paid one tranche to Staughton's instructions.'

Eric was beginning to see the picture. 'A sum of money which had never been received by Malaysia Mobile.'

'Exactly. Or so they say.' Lintern managed a grim smile. 'Classic, isn't it? But their problem, not ours.'

'How would you reach that conclusion?' Eric asked cautiously.

'It doesn't matter a damn whether Staughton took it to the board or not. He *told* us he had. And he was speaking as a Vice President of Malaysia Mobile. He was holding himself out as having the authority, and as far as we are concerned, that's good enough. We can't be bound by any secret arrangements they have in the company. We can't be expected to know about that, can we? I believe,' Lintern said, sarcastically, 'you lawyers call it the Rule in *Turquand's Case*.'

Eric nodded. Ocean Distribution were not legally required to inquire into the regularity of another company's internal proceedings—which might relate to restrictions on the authority of one of their directors to enter contracts. Lintern had a point.

'As far as we're concerned, I struck a deal with the Vice President of Malaysia Mobile. He seemed to us to have authority to strike such a deal. The fact that he absconded with the money thereafter isn't our problem. We've paid over part of the purchase price, but the sale was in any case conditional upon a three-year charter. The fact is, Chan doesn't want to pay the fixed charter rates for the *Arctic Queen*—I mean, rates have gone down with a thump, but we'd agreed a fixed rate on all three charters. And he wants the full price for the damned ship. Well, he can't have one thing without the other. We're prepared to pay what we owe—which does not include the money taken by Staughton—but we also want them to honour the three one-year charters. Alternatively, if they won't honour the deal, we want our money back on the sale—whether Staughton ever handed it over to Malaysia Mobile or not.' He eyed Eric speculatively. 'And that's where we are at the moment.'

'Malaysia Mobile are sticking?'

'Chan is obdurate. I can't get past him to his board. All conversations and communications are with him. I suspect he's scared of having the whole thing exposed. But he's got no choice. We've instructed our lawyers. There's a lot of money at stake. There'll be no damn change out of eight million—and that's before we pay the lawyers' fees!'

His tone had become more heated. Eric watched him, saw the anger stirring in his eyes and the set of his mouth and wondered whether Simon Chan and Paul Lintern might have something in common. It was likely that Simon Chan was not the only one with his head on the block: it seemed to Eric that if Paul Lintern didn't win this litigation, his future in Ocean Distribution would be short and brutish.

'I've nothing against Simon Chan personally, of course,' Lintern said, banking down his fires. 'He's not to blame here—he's merely covering his back. He didn't know about the arrangements, apparently, nor did his board. He was conned by Harry Staughton, just as much as I was. But my back is covered—I've got the agreements, and I've got the law to support me. But I can understand why Chan would engage you to find Harry Staughton. He's got some explaining to do to Chan and the board. He's the key to all this. Indeed . . .' His eyes were hooded again, as he reflected. 'I wonder . . . is there any reason why you and I couldn't also come to some . . . arrangement?'

'I don't understand.'

'I have an interest in finding Staughton also. He would be a key witness for us. If I could find him, get him on the stand . . .' His glance dwelled on Eric.

'I've already got an assignment,' Eric said firmly. 'I'm working for Simon Chan. I couldn't accept a commission which might conflict with that.'

'Parallel lines, not conflict,' Lintern murmured. 'However, no matter. I am sure that if you do discover the whereabouts of our villainous Mr Staughton, Simon Chan will know what to do with him. And as far as the litigation is concerned, I don't think Staughton could lie his way out of the situation, even under pressure from Chan and Malaysia Mobile. The issue of the money, after all, is their problem. Staughton defrauded Malaysia Mobile, not Ocean Distribution, when he walked away with the first tranche of our payment for the *Arctic Queen*. No, their interest in Harry Staughton is greater than mine. I hope you find him, Mr Ward, and bring him to justice so that we also can extract out of him what we want. But in the long term, it matters little. We can't lose. We shall proceed, with or without Staughton.'

'I presume you've got the relevant documentation that would allow you to make your case without Staughton?'

'We have. And, well, there's also that man Reynolds. Yes . . . there's always Reynolds.' Lintern smiled thinly, his eyes watchful. 'So to that extent, to hell with Harry Staughton, wherever he may be.'

He rose, putting down his glass and said goodbye,

abruptly. He walked away to collect his coat: upright, committed, powerful in his righteousness.

Eric was left with the impression, nevertheless, that Paul Lintern was not as dismissive as he wanted to appear: it mattered to him very much where Harry Staughton might be. Whatever impression he might want to give, Paul Lintern was urgent in his desire to get his teeth into the man who had made a fool of him over the sale of the *Arctic Queen*.

3

It was early morning and the beach at Granadella was deserted. The pebbles rasped and clattered under Arturo's feet as he clambered past the beached boats and began to climb over the rocks, the morning sun hot on the back of his neck as it rose above Cabo la Não.

He scrambled over the smooth plateau of limestone where late-night revellers had held a barbecue, kicking aside the blackened wood embers as he passed. The crags loomed up ahead of him: it was not an easy climb, but for someone as young and agile as he it was possible. The advantage was that when others came down to the beach they would not follow: clumsy, corpulent, lazy, they did not know of his own special place around the headland, where he could be alone and silent. There he could sit and listen only to the crash of the waves on the rocks while he dreamed and fished and waited to grow into a man. Then he would have his own boat, and sail off across the blue sea, beyond the island of Descrubidor, the Discoverer, the craggy rock from which one of Columbus's navigators had sailed, centuries ago.

Arturo carried his fishing-rod across his shoulder. It was a prized possession—a tourist discard that he had managed to scrounge outside the market last year. It had brought him success, and good luck: he fished well, and profitably, for here under the sea-lashed headland big fish lurked, away from the boats of Granadella beach.

He found his usual perch, the flat stone supporting his back and giving him shelter later in the day, the sun climbing high in the sky, and he cast his line. In the deep distance he could hear the drone of an unseen flight from Alicante, far to the south. The sea was glassy, smooth, lifting in long green-blue swell, and down there the fish would be lurking. He sat and dreamed, and the sun slipped higher in the aching blue of the sky.

He dreamed. And in a little while, he slept.

The gentle pull on his line brought him back to a sharp awakening. His line was taut: he had hooked something big, but it was lazy, it was not fighting, the hook could not have bitten deep. Carefully he played the line, but there was still no battle, no struggling in the deep water.

But it was heavy.

A light breeze arose from the sea, lifting the swell, and Arturo hauled in his line. He was puzzled, at a loss to understand what he had hooked. Then he saw the dark back, slick and wet, and he stood up. The shiny surface, discoloured, was like no fish he had seen. Then the swell rolled it forward and he saw the bloated features, the sightless, hollowed-out eyes in the face.

'*Madre de Dios*,' he exclaimed.

He dropped his line and ran.

CHAPTER 4

1

The forecast for the weekend had been good and Anne was due to visit Alnwick to have a meeting with the county surveyor on Friday afternoon so she persuaded Eric it would be a good idea to take the weekend off—get away from Sedleigh Hall as well as work. They had both been busy of late and had had little time for each other. The break would do them good.

Eric agreed, particularly since Leonard Channing had called another meeting of the board early the following week, so Eric would have to go to London again.

Once Anne's meeting with the county surveyor in Alnwick was over Eric picked her up in Narrowgate and drove north out of the town, over the old Lion Bridge and on to the A1. The traffic was surprisingly light and they made good progress until they turned off left towards Elwick and Easington Grange.

They found a small inn where they were able to obtain a room for the night. The bill of fare was surprisingly good and they retired early. In the morning they headed for Ross Bach Sands.

It was familiar to Anne, but Eric had never been there before. They left the car and walked across the sands, a glorious four-mile sweep of beach, towards the nature reserve at Budle Bay. There they were able to climb the road to the crest that gave them a distant view of Lindisfarne, then walk across a narrow strip of farmland until they were able to see the arrogant pile of Bamburgh Castle dominating the seascape, with the dark waves rolling in at its foot.

When they returned to the car they were both hungry so they drove to Seahouses for a light snack in the pub there. They then decided to drive on further north-west, towards the Border Forests. It would take them in a long loop on a homeward track to Sedleigh Hall.

When they finally got back, after tramping over the hills and feeling the fresh, sea-tanged air in their nostrils, they were both refreshed by having spoken nothing about business throughout the whole weekend. It had been a way of recharging their professional and personal batteries.

They hadn't even seen a newspaper.

*

Newcastle, and the Quayside, presented a contrast. There had been a breakdown on the Tyne Bridge itself, and the traffic had built up, both south and northward into the city, so Eric had difficulty getting in to the office. There were various matters on his desk that he had to deal with personally, and his secretary had a message from Simon Chan for him.

'He says he would like to meet you urgently. Unfortunately he can't get up north, but he is in London until Thursday.'

'That's fine,' Eric said. 'Get back to his secretary and arrange a meeting at my club on Tuesday evening. I'm down in London for the Martin and Channing board, anyway.'

He was able to get the five o'clock train south, and was in his club shortly after 8.0 p.m., to have a quiet dinner.

Leonard Channing had called the board meeting for 10.30 in the morning. Eric was there in good time and indulged in desultory conversation with two other members of the board before the chairman arrived.

Leonard Channing started the meeting promptly.

'Well, gentlemen, there are several items we need to deal with quickly this morning. First on the agenda is the Taylor Trust. Sir Harry, can you speak on that?'

The meeting moved on smoothly. Eric had little part to play and contented himself with listening. By midday they were nearing the end of the agenda. Leonard Channing paused, and pursed his lips. 'We come to any other business,' he said, almost purring. 'I thought it might be an appropriate time to ask Eric for a report on the Iberica bid to take over Artaros.'

Eric sat up in surprise. 'I understand you had previously ruled that items not appearing on the agenda could not be taken.'

'Chairman's privilege,' Channing said smugly. 'And I think the board would agree the matter is important.'

There were nods of assent. When Eric looked around, no one met his glance. Eric realized the item had not been unexpected—other than by him.

'There's not a great deal I can say,' he began, 'other than to give you a rundown on the state of the stocks, the positioning of Iberica in the market, and the tactics which Artaros are insisting upon—'

'Well, maybe we can start with that,' Sir Harry Sims broke in. An ex-Army officer, and Vice Chairman of Martin and Channing, he tended to take the party line on most matters and was a close confidant of Leonard Channing. His moustache almost seemed to bristle with indignation as he went on, 'We've all seen the financial papers this last week—and I consider that's what we find most disturbing. There was an article by a man called Cooper which was really little more than a muck-raking attack on Coleman.'

'The documentation to support it is available,' Eric replied.

'That's not the point. The issue here is whether or not Martin and Channing should allow themselves to be involved in such a tactic.'

Eric waited. Leonard Channing said nothing, leaning back in his chair innocently, tips of his fingers placed precisely together, presiding over the board with a gentle hand. 'The tactics are the direct result of instructions from the Chief Executive of Artaros,' Eric said.

'It smacks of dirty tricks. Coleman may be a corporate raider, but we're a respectable institution with a name to protect,' Sir Harry expostulated. He had clearly been put up as front line troops by the Chairman. 'I think we should be more inclined to insist on a change of tactics, rather than tamely go along with what Artaros demand. After all, they're paying us—'

'Exactly,' Eric replied. 'And they're very committed to the tactics you deplore. Should we then withdraw, and lose the commission?'

'Oh, come on, Ward, that's an admission of defeat.'

'It's a practical alternative. Artaros are insistent. And our Chairman, incidentally, *was* in Singapore.'

'I was not exactly party to the full discussions,' Leonard Channing suggested quickly.

'Because you chose to absent yourself, Chairman. And you should have been aware of the way things were likely to go. But I have an open mind. I would have no objection if the board saw fit to find someone else to handle the matter in a more . . . acceptable way. I would be happy to relinquish control of the defence—hand over to one of you.'

There was a long silence. Then they all began to speak at once.

It was all as Eric had guessed, of course. Reputation was one thing; losing a hefty commission in a takeover bid—where Martin and Channing would win whichever side lost in the battle—was another. The argument had raged until almost 1.30, but the result had always been a foregone conclusion as far as Eric was concerned.

Leonard Channing had summed it up.

'The general feeling is one of unhappiness. We hope that the . . . ah . . . tone of the defence will be changed. We leave that in your hands, and ask that you apply your best judgement to it. The board is convinced that now you've started, you should continue . . . but care should be exercised.'

In other words, the warning was on the wall in six foot letters. He was to remain in charge of the operation; he was to be careful; they would not give up the commission; and any mud that was flung would stick to Eric Ward, and not to Leonard Channing or the board members. They would have minutes which effectively made that clear.

They had their scapegoat, and they were keeping the commission. They were happy. And Channing was even happier—he'd got exactly what he wanted out of the meeting.

*

Eric took the opportunity to spend the afternoon with the solicitors who acted as his London agents in Lincoln's Inn Fields. It was five o'clock before he left them and made his way back to the club. He read in the library for a while, then bathed and changed, in time to meet Simon Chan in the Members' Lounge on the first floor.

Chan was shown up precisely on time. Eric offered him a drink, was not surprised to learn it would be a brandy, and placed the order with the waiter.

Chan made polite inquiries about Anne and the state of Eric's business until the drinks arrived. Then, taking his from the proffered tray, he said abruptly, 'It would seem I engaged your services a little late in the day, Mr Ward.'

'How do you mean?'

'You did not see the newspapers on Saturday?'

Eric shook his head. 'Anne and I went walking at the weekend. We didn't really get around to—'

'A pity. However, I have a cutting.' He produced a neatly clipped piece of newspaper from his wallet, unfolded it and handed it over to Eric.

MYSTERY DEATH IN SPAIN

The body of an unidentified man was discovered off Granadella Beach on Tuesday morning by a young boy fishing from the headland. While early statements suggested it might have been an accidental drowning, later comments emanating from the local police headquarters suggested that a violent death was more likely. The possibility of a shooting was not ruled out by police spokesmen.

Clothing found on the body lead the police to believe the dead man was English in origin. The state of the body, having been immersed in water for some time, has made the task of identification difficult, and the police have been making inquiries with regard to missing persons in the area. Latest reports suggest, however, that the incident may well be linked to the disappearance of a Mr and Mrs Suffolk from an isolated villa on the hills near Alta Marina . . .

Eric looked at Simon Chan. 'I don't see—'

'At the weekend there was no identification made. But on Sunday night the name was released positively: Peter Suffolk. By ten on Monday morning my informants tell me that it is likely that the man was shot to death. They also inform me the passport in the name of Suffolk was a forgery. Interpol are now alerted.'

'I still don't understand.'

'I think the man found in the sea was Harry Staughton. Your quest, Mr Ward, is over.'

'How can you be sure?' Eric asked, puzzled.

Simon Chan shrugged, and sipped his drink. 'I explained to you. I have contacts . . . a good network. I wanted you to investigate the north-east connections. I have also approached other people. The descriptions that have been furnished to me . . . the length of time the Suffolks have been at the villa . . . I am fairly certain that the dead man is the man I was looking for.'

'When would you expect to get confirmation?'

'There is a possibility a public announcement will be made within a day or so.' He sighed. 'This complicates things, of course . . . but perhaps it also makes matters a little simpler.'

'You'll have to report it to your board?'

'Of course. But I expect less trouble from them now. The Chinese are an odd people, Mr Ward—death binds them together in a way you would not understand. We honour our dead—we do not seek to revile them. There will be no attempt to besmirch the memory of Harry Staughton. Rather, the board—even my Malaysian Vice Chairman—will now seek to rally around and try to do what is best for Malaysia Mobile.'

'You think the fraud issue will just be swept under the carpet?'

'Hardly that. In other spheres it is called damage limitation. There is nothing to be gained by pursuing the matter. We write off the loss—and attempt to achieve the best result we can in the circumstances.' Simon Chan watched Eric with narrowed eyes, careful as a prowling cat. 'The fraud is not public knowledge, of course. And any information you will have received is privileged—the client's privilege, if I understand English law.'

'You're quite correct,' Eric said stiffly. 'I shall disclose nothing. But Ocean Distribution will draw attention to it.'

'Of course. You have been speaking to Paul Lintern.' Chan nodded wisely. 'Yes, the . . . ah . . . alleged fraudulent behaviour of Harry Staughton, now deceased, it will be part of their case . . . but that will be very difficult to prove if they have no personal testimony to support the issue. And with Staughton dead, and conflicting documentation which proves neither one thing nor another, their case is weakened.'

Eric looked at Chan carefully. In a casual tone, he said, 'So, in a sense, it perhaps suits you better that Staughton is dead?'

Simon Chan permitted himself a thin smile. 'That is rather a direct way of putting it, Mr Ward, but I suppose your statement has a certain logic about it.' He paused. 'However, it is over. Harry Staughton has been . . . removed from the scene. I am in a position now to say that I, and my company, no longer require your services. Perhaps we could discuss the matter of your fee over dinner?'

They ate in relative silence. Eric was preoccupied with his own thoughts, and Simon Chan seemed content to eat and drink and surreptitiously observe the behaviour of other diners in the room. Chan asked Eric his impressions on Singapore, and advised him that he should visit Kuala Lumpur, if only to observe the accommodation that Christianity and the Muslim faith had reached, in their buildings and their business. 'It is said we have there a mosque that looks like a railway station, and a railway station that looks like a mosque,' Chan added, smiling.

'Both will enable you to travel long distances.'

'Physically with the one,' Chan nodded, 'and spiritually with the other.'

'So,' Eric said with a sigh, 'what will now happen over your litigation with Ocean Distribution?'

Simon Chan hesitated. He glanced around the room and shrugged slightly. 'Paul Lintern is an angry man. I think he is subject to . . . pressures, similar to those I have experienced of recent months.'

'So you think he'll press on?'

'Compromise in such circumstances is difficult. No, it is clear to me that Mr Lintern will press his case, and do so firmly.' He paused. 'As I have said, his case becomes less tenable with the death of Harry Staughton. There would always have been the possibility that Staughton would turn coat, do some sort of deal with Lintern if it came to court. Now, the situation has changed, radically.' He smiled, but there was no light of humour in his narrow eyes. 'So the boot changes feet, as you say. Now, it is we who will be pressing ahead.'

'How do you mean?'

Simon Chan gazed at him blandly. 'If Lintern continues, we will be making a counter-claim. And if he withdraws, we will in any case be joining issue with him as claimants in our own right.'

Eric leaned back in his chair. 'On what grounds would you go ahead? What would your argument be?'

Chan hesitated. 'Paul Lintern entered an agreement, he claims, with Harry Staughton. The fact is, Staughton had no authority to enter such an agreement—and Lintern either was, or should have been put, on notice of that fact. Indeed, the advice I have taken would suggest we should be proceeding not simply along the lines of a recovery of the full price for the *Arctic Queen*. We should also be seeking damages.'

'Damages?' Eric raised his eyebrows. 'For what?'

'Conspiracy.'

'I'm afraid I don't follow,' Eric said.

'It has become clear to me that we are not simply dealing here with the aberrations of one man—Harry Staughton. If we look at the behaviour of the people involved, there is just too much activity which one can describe as being based on naïvété . . . or negligence.'

'Negligence doesn't amount to conspiracy.'

'True.' Chan smiled benignly. 'But if we take that one further step and consider whether the activity was not negligent but deliberate, perhaps we reach the realm of the offence I am talking about.'

'So you'll be proceeding not simply against Ocean Distribution, then?'

'Against Ocean Distribution for full payment under the contract of sale for the *Arctic Queen*. But against Paul Lintern for fraud and conspiracy.'

'You need more than one to raise a charge of conspiracy.'

'Apart from Lintern, you mean? There is a dead conspirator.'

'Harry Staughton?'

Chan smiled, and nodded. 'And there could be another. That one could prove the weak link in the chain, as far as Lintern is concerned,' he said quietly. He was silent for a little while, then he gazed directly at Eric. 'I did have it in mind to ask you to prepare the papers for the case.'

'Not really my scene, Mr Chan. I'm not a corporate lawyer.'

'Though a man of parts. Yes . . . I say I thought of you. In the event I decided otherwise. There is a man who has come to my attention . . . I am impressed by him, and by his firm. He is, of course, known to you.'

'I know a lot of lawyers.'

'This one you know well—as does your wife. I have decided to instruct Mr Charles Davison.'

All in all, Eric thought to himself, this had not been one of his better days.

2

Eric had maintained his contacts with the police both in Northumberland and Durham. There were men in both forces he kept well clear of, but there were others who had retained a wary friendship with him. The relationships could have been closer but for the fact that there were occasions when Eric appeared against the police in court—and some regarded solicitors as anathema.

Tony O'Connor was different. He was considerably younger than Eric, and had just been making his way in the force when Eric had tendered his resignation on account of glaucoma. They had struck up a friendly relationship, however, partly as a result of one particularly violent night in the West End when O'Connor and Eric had faced a group of drunken Scots armed with broken beer bottles. They had come out of it with a mutual trust and respect, even though it had not led to a close friendship. O'Connor was now a detective-inspector, based at Wallsend. He was amenable to the suggestion that he meet Eric for a drink in Newcastle.

They chose a quiet pub on the outskirts of the town. The Dog and Engine was rather elderly in its appearance—square, squat, uncompromising in its position on the roundabout, it tended to draw crowds of youngsters at weekends because of the Geordie rock group that played there on Saturday nights, but during the week it was fairly empty.

Eric was already standing at the bar when O'Connor came in. He was a big, untidy man with red hair and a broad, splayed nose—the result of a rugby injury. He played in the second row for one of the Gosforth teams and had a certain reputation for what he called commitment, and what others described as rough-housing. He was a cheerful man with twinkling eyes and a Newcastle accent.

'You dinna bring your badge this time, then, Eric, hey?'

'Badge?'

'Why, aye, you know—the one that says "You can trust me, I'm a lawyer."' O'Connor chuckled and banged a meaty fist on the bar. 'Mine's a pint.'

'Newcastle Brown?'

'What else, man? Missus well, is she?'

'Very.'

O'Connor turned, leaning against the bar to survey the half-empty room. 'Not much life here during the week, bonny lad.'

'All the better for quiet conversations.'

O'Connor glanced at Eric and smiled. 'Oh aye. Not just a social chat, then.'

'You know I'm always pleased to buy you a pint,' Eric replied, with a grin.

'If it buys you some information,' O'Connor said. 'But it's a good pint and you've done me favours in the past, so what's it about?'

'Shall we sit down?' Eric gestured towards a table near the window. O'Connor led the way, thrusting his burly frame past a small group of middle-aged men gathered near the dartboard. He sat down heavily and took a long pull at his beer. 'So . . . talk to me.'

Eric hesitated. 'I don't know whether you can help, really. There was an item in the weekend papers. A man killed in Spain. The newspapers named him as Peter Suffolk.'

'Oh aye.' O'Connor lowered his head so Eric was unable to see his eyes. 'What about it?'

'I have a client . . . who's been talking to me about the case. But my client has information to suggest the name Suffolk was a false one. Forged passport.'

There was a shout from the men at the dartboard as one

of them completed a successful series. O'Connor scowled at them, then turned back to Eric. 'Got inside tracks then, has he, your client?'

Eric shrugged. 'I don't know where he got the information. But yes, it seems he has a . . . network.'

'Don't we all,' O'Connor said moodily. 'And what else did this . . . client tell you?'

'He says the man's real name was Harry Staughton, the former Vice President and Charter Manager of Malaysia Mobile, who disappeared some while ago.'

'Is that so, now?' A thoughtful expression came over O'Connor's heavy face. He traced a finger around the rim of his beer glass. 'And what's your client's interest in this Staughton character?'

'It's ended, now he's dead.'

'But yours hasn't.'

Eric shrugged. 'I suppose it has, really. But I don't like loose ends. I just wondered whether you'd heard anything . . . or could confirm what my client told me.'

O'Connor pulled a face, and scratched at the red thatch of hair. He rested his chin on his hand. 'Confirm? Well, no reason why I shouldn't do that, is there? I'm not givin' away information after all, and you are an old mucker . . . Yeah, your client has a network all right. Suffolk was a pseudonym, as they say: the guy's real name is Staughton, and Interpol have been lookin' into the business. They've been in touch—'

'Because Staughton has north-eastern connections?'

O'Connor's eyes widened. 'You *have* been doing your homework! Aye, he was a Sunderland lad, so they asked us to check him out.'

'I don't think you'll find much,' Eric suggested. 'He behaved himself when he lived up here.'

'Is that right? But he hasn't since, obviously. What do you know about this guy, Eric?'

Without naming Simon Chan, or explaining the reason for his own investigations, Eric sketched out what he knew about Harry Staughton. O'Connor pursed his lips. 'Well, well . . . that's more than we knew. Useful . . . So the guy was a con man, hey? It's a road we've not been goin' down, but it's early days. I mean, at this time all we're doin' is getting background stuff. Interpol are co-ordinating the investigation with the Spanish police. On the other hand . . .'

Eric waited.

'We've been asked about someone else, as well. I can't tell you too much, you understand. But Interpol have put out a trace on a guy they think might be connected with some credit card frauds. They don't know for certain there's a connection, but this character has been movin' through Europe leaving a long trail of unpaid bills, and some of them turned up in the area where Staughton was turned off. Since this guy has Newcastle connections also, we've been asked to keep an eye open for him.'

'I see.' Eric hesitated. 'Anything else?'

O'Connor frowned into his beer. 'It's all a bit sketchy, really. I mean, we're on the fringe of it all, up here, you knaa. You tell me the guy was a con man who skipped when things got hot for him. That's interesting. Fills in the reasons, which Interpol haven't mentioned to us. But what we have been told is that Staughton wasn't alone—there was a woman with him at the villa—and she's disappeared. Whether she ended up the same way as Staughton, we don't know. And then, well, the guy who put a bullet into Staughton—and there was just one bullet, by the way, straight in the head, clean professional job—was looking for something. Seems he turned over the villa.'

'Anything missing?'

'Who can tell? All we know is this guy must have broken into the house, done in Staughton and maybe the woman with him, found—or didn't find—what he was looking for, and scarpered. We've been asked to keep our eyes open. Any help as far as you're concerned?'

*

It had been mainly curiosity which had taken Eric to Tony O'Connor. His involvement with the Staughton case was now really at an end. Simon Chan had engaged him to find Staughton, but now that the man was dead, Chan had withdrawn the assignment and his retainer of Eric was over.

Eric was disturbed, nevertheless. The abrupt termination of the manhunt was logical and sensible, of course, but Chan's attitude towards the issue behind Staughton's disappearance rang hollow in some way. He now seemed to feel he would have no further trouble from his board, and that surprised Eric. It made him wonder whether the tale about a thrusting Malaysian Vice Chairman had been a gloss upon the truth.

And Staughton's death certainly seemed to have lifted an anxiety from Simon Chan.

On the other hand, he thought, as he stood at the window of his office, staring out over the bustle on the Quayside where a freighter destined for Denmark was loading, his involvement was now over. He had other things to get on with . . . not least the Iberica business. But he couldn't help wondering whether Simon Chan would now ever do a deal with Morcomb Enterprises and even Sir Henry Slocum and his Teesside developments. It was possible Chan's visit to the north had really been connected simply with his hunt for Harry Staughton, and the rest of it had just been cover.

Cover . . . Eric shook his head. He was getting fanciful. It came of working in a world where everyone seemed to be wriggling to obtain some sort of advantage: Leonard Channing, Greg Bowles, Paul Lintern, Matt Coleman, Simon Chan, Harry Staughton himself—all scurrying around like rats, trying to take the biggest bite of the cake.

And it was a world he, Eric Ward, was getting more and more bound up in. Maybe it was time to get out. Maybe Anne was right, when she said they could have a better life if he worked with her for Morcomb Enterprises.

The telephone on his desk buzzed. Eric walked across the room and picked it up.

'Mr Ward? There's someone in reception who is asking to see you.'

Eric glanced at his appointments book. 'I'm expecting no one.'

'He's come in on the chance he can see you. Personally.'

'What's it about?'

There was a muffled sound, a hand over the receiver, and a short delay. The receptionist came back on. 'The gentleman says it's a confidential matter, which he wants to talk to you about in private. He says his name is Reynolds.'

Eric frowned. 'Les Reynolds?'

'That's right, Mr Ward.'

Eric hesitated. 'All right. You'd better show him up.'

It seemed as though his escape from the affairs of Harry Staughton was not going to be so easy, after all.

3

Les Reynolds was nervous.

He was wearing a brown jacket and white shirt and the collar seemed too tight. His face was flushed and he was sweating, his cropped sandy hair damp. Some of the bubbling enthusiasm had gone from his personality and he appeared ill at ease, and concerned. His movements were jerky and his hands shaky: he presented quite a different appearance from the self-confident man Eric had met at Plymouth.

'Sit down, Mr Reynolds. Can I offer you anything?'

'A cup of coffee would be fine.' Les Reynolds licked his lips. 'I'm grateful that you can see me at such short notice.'

'I hope I can help,' Eric said. He buzzed the secretary downstairs and arranged for two cups of coffee to be brought in. 'Are you in Newcastle on business?'

Reynolds nodded nervously. 'That's right. I had to get up here to . . . to see someone. You know . . . you know Cartwright Shipping?'

Eric shook his head. 'The Gateshead firm? I've had no dealings with them.'

'I had to see someone there. I was in town for a couple of days. When I'm away like this, I usually ring in to the London office to see if anything's cropped up.'

'Something has?'

Reynolds twisted in his chair as the door opened and Eric's secretary brought in the coffees. He waited until the girl had left and then sipped at the coffee. 'You could say that. You get away from the office for a couple of days and trouble always arrives. I was up here . . . I thought I'd better see you about it at once.'

'What did it concern?' Eric asked.

Reynolds hesitated, uncertain for a moment. 'Are you still representing Simon Chan?'

'No. The search for Harry Staughton has been called off.'

Reynolds leaned back in his chair, and sighed. 'That's a relief. When we talked last time . . . I thought . . . well, you remember I said maybe there'd be a time when you could help me. As it happens, it looks like the time's come.'

'In what way?'

'I phoned in to the office in London. There's a writ been served. A copy arrived for me this afternoon. Malaysia Mobile are suing International Charters and Ocean Distribution. It's not just that they're defending the attack from Paul Lintern. They're going on to the charge themselves—and they've named me as a co-defendant!'

Eric frowned. He recalled now what Simon Chan had said at their last meeting. Chan had mentioned that there might be someone else to proceed against. 'You'd better give me the full story,' he said quietly.

'I don't know it!' Reynolds almost wailed the words. 'Why the hell should he join me in the action? I tell you, I was just a bystander in the whole thing.'

'Let's start at the beginning,' Eric suggested.

Reynolds shrugged despondently. 'You know some of it

already. It's all about the bloody *Arctic Queen*. Damn Harry Staughton! I wish I'd never met him.'

'I gather you wouldn't be alone in that.'

'Too damn right! Anyway, I told you Staughton negotiated the sale of the ship through me from Artaros—that's when we met, really. After that, he used us to do the deal with Ocean Distribution. But that's all it ever was! I was friendly with Harry, sure—he was a great guy to be with. But that was all there was to it. I met Paul Lintern, I set up the arrangements, and for that there was a commission payable. A commission I never bloody well got.'

'So what's the substance of the claim against you?' Eric asked.

Reynolds shook his head. 'It's crazy! Look, I never knew what was going on, I swear. It was all nothing to do with me—I just acted on Staughton's instructions. In the first instance, he said it was to be a straight sale. Then Paul Lintern came back and told me it was no go unless there could be a guaranteed charter of some kind. At that stage I brought the two parties together.'

'Were you present at their meeting?'

'Of course. I was handling the negotiations.' Reynolds ran a nervous hand over his chin. 'And it was all pretty straightforward stuff, believe me. Lintern said he'd have to have a charter agreement. Harry said he'd do his best to fix one. Then he came up with the thought that Malaysia Mobile themselves would take a charter.'

'Did that surprise you?'

Reynolds grimaced. 'Not really. Staughton explained it simply enough at the time. Malaysia Mobile had bought the ship under the option arrangement from Artaros, with the intention of chartering on, but they had developed uses for the vessel themselves, in the Indian Ocean trade. They'd be happy to recoup some of their investment on the sale, but in the meanwhile, with their own commitments out of Calcutta, they'd be happy enough to charter back provided the rates were acceptable.'

'And were they?'

'They proved to be a bit of a sticking-point. Indeed, at one stage I thought the thing would fall through. You got to remember, charter rates worldwide were dropping. Anyway, they finally hit on an agreement—a fixed rate of £350,000 a month.'

'Was that a reasonable rate?'

'Maybe a bit on the high side,' Reynolds admitted cautiously. 'I told Harry so. But in the end he agreed it. And that's when Lintern really put the boot in.'

'The term of the charter?'

Reynolds stared at him uncertainly. 'You heard about this?'

'Simon Chan gave me some background . . . before we parted company,' Eric explained.

'So you know Lintern demanded a three-year charter. I mean, that was a bugger, believe me! A fixed rate for three years, at a time when charter rates were slipping. Harry argued, but in the end gave way. He said he'd have to go back to the board to get their agreement, but he'd do his best.'

'What happened then?'

Reynolds ran his tongue over dry lips. He sipped at his coffee. 'It was well over a fortnight later that Harry got in touch with me. He told me to set up a meeting with Paul Lintern. He'd got an agreement from his board. I did what he asked.'

'Just what did Staughton present to Lintern as an agreement?'

'I don't know.' Reynolds shook his head. 'It was at that stage that I was shut out. You see, Harry came back and said a three-year charter would be OK and he asked me to set up the necessary documentation. While I was making the necessary arrangements, he said, he wanted a private word with Lintern.'

'What about?'

'I don't know. When I came back into the discussion—

it took me about an hour to get a draft together—they'd finished their little talk, and they seemed all amicable. It was like they'd become buddies suddenly.'

'So you don't know what deal had been struck between the two of them?'

Reynolds shook his head. 'I've told you exactly what I set up.'

Eric hesitated. 'You had no inkling that they might have agreed upon some . . . variation of the agreement you had negotiated?'

'I told you. They seemed at ease with each other and we went ahead with the agreement.'

'You saw no other documentation?'

'What else was there to see?'

Eric rose and walked across to the window again, to stare out at the Danish freighter. They had almost completed the loading now: she should be proceeding down river on the evening tide, swinging out towards Tynemouth and the open sea twelve miles away. He turned to look at Reynolds. 'I had a conversation with Paul Lintern the other day. He's an angry, bitter man.'

'So?'

'His account has it that Staughton came back with a provision: he insisted that the three-year charter wasn't on, unless it could be done with three one-year-long consecutive charters. Was that the documentation you completed?'

Reynolds frowned, puzzled. 'No. I just did a three-year charter, as such. I heard there was a dispute between Ocean Distribution and Malaysia Mobile, but are you telling me that Chan and Lintern are actually arguing over the terms of the charter?'

'Staughton told Lintern, it seems, that his board would agree three years but only on one-year charters, for private, Malaysian tax reasons. Lintern apparently went along with that.' Eric paused, watching Reynolds carefully. 'And you didn't draft that agreement?'

'I did not! I knew nothing about any such variation! As

far as I was concerned, the deal went through on a straight basis. Whatever variation was made, it certainly wasn't negotiated by me.'

'So you weren't involved in any other documentation regarding the charters?'

'I didn't even know there *was* any other documentation.'

Eric was silent. He stared at Les Reynolds. The man was quieter now, more confident, less ill at ease, as though the opportunity to talk about his troubles had calmed him, enabled him to settle. Eric had seen the reaction before: talking to a solicitor could be like handing the problem over to someone else. It was cathartic for some people.

'The writ that's been served on Ocean Distribution—what's the claim?'

'Fraud, and conspiracy. It's a try-on, Mr Ward, and it'll ruin me. I'll make no bones about it. International Charters isn't a big business. And we're talking of a suit for damages of eight million, for God's sake! If Chan pins any of this mess on me, I'll be flat broke! And I know damn-all about it. I was just a commission agent. I was conned by Harry Staughton as much as Chan was, and for all I know, Lintern as well. That's why I've come to you. I want you to represent me. I want you to defend this action. You've had dealings with Chan. You know all about this business. Will you take me on?'

Eric hesitated. He was not certain that he really wanted to get further involved in the life and death of Harry Staughton. On the other hand, Simon Chan had engaged the services of none other than Charles Davison to represent him. The temptation was too great. Eric nodded. 'Yes, Mr Reynolds, I'll prepare your defence.'

Reynolds leaned back in his chair. He looked relieved. He managed a smile. 'I'm glad of that, Mr Ward. I tell you, when the office told me about that writ . . .' He leaned forward, and finished his coffee. 'Anyway, you'll let me know what papers you'll want and all that sort of thing.'

'We'll need another conference. Probably in your office.

I'll need to have access to all documentation held by you in relation to your dealings with Harry Staughton. I wouldn't want anything suddenly turning up which might prove on the day to be . . . embarrassing.'

Reynolds grinned. 'That won't happen, Mr Ward. I've come clean with you. You can have the lot.' He stood up, ready to go. He looked directly at Eric. 'Talking of Harry Staughton . . . I was surprised by this writ in the sense that Chan is going for Lintern and me. There's no mention of Harry. And you tell me he's ended your retainer to find the bastard. Does that mean he's given up on Harry Staughton?'

Eric was silent for several seconds. 'Harry Staughton is dead, Mr Reynolds.'

'*What?*' Les Reynolds stared at Eric, his mouth wide open as though he was gasping for breath. There was a panic-stricken look in his eyes. '*How the hell do you know that?*'

'It isn't public knowledge yet, but it soon will be. He was murdered. In Spain. He was using a false name. He—'

Reynolds's legs were giving way under him. He sat down again, abruptly. He stared at Eric but he hardly saw him: unreadable emotions chased across his face and all the anxieties he had displayed earlier were back. 'Hell's flames,' he muttered. 'Hell's flames . . .'

'Are you all right?' Eric asked, concerned. The man had taken the news badly. He was shaking slightly and his eyes were staring, almost scared.

He put his hands on the desk in front of him. He stared at them, gradually regaining control. 'That's a shaker, Mr Ward. OK, he conned me, but . . . but I liked him.'

'I'm sorry. I was too abrupt. You sure you're going to be all right?'

Reynolds nodded. After a moment, he rose. 'I'll be OK. It's just that . . . it was a shaker . . . I didn't know . . . I'll be in touch, Mr Ward.' He walked slowly from the room, still unnerved, his cheeks pale.

As the door closed behind him the telephone rang. It was reception. 'Sorry to bother you, Mr Ward, but there's a call for you.'

'That's all right. I'll take it. I'm alone—Mr Reynolds is on the way down. See him out, please.'

He waited while the call was transferred.

'Is your name Ward?' It was a woman's voice. It was sharp, edgy, lacking in control.

'That's right.'

'I need to see you. A . . . a friend recommended you.'

'I'm flattered, but what is it about?'

She sounded nervous, her breathing rasping in the phone. 'I can't talk over the phone like this. But I need help . . . I want you to meet me.'

'Well, if you'd like to make an appointment to call in here to see me at the office—'

'That's not possible!'

'I'm sorry, but—'

'Don't you understand? This is important. It's urgent.' She hesitated, clearly reluctant to be specific over the phone. 'It's about Harry Staughton.'

Eric was silent for a few seconds. He frowned, puzzled. 'Just who is this?'

'I'm in Berwick. I'm in a safe house. You must meet me there. I need protection. Please come.'

'I'm sorry,' Eric replied, somewhat irritated. 'I can't just go driving up to Berwick—who is this?'

'My name is Leah Bowles. I've got to talk to you. Will you come?'

Bowles . . . Eric shook his head angrily. 'Berwick is a long way, Mrs Bowles.'

'Four-thirty tomorrow. Please. I'll meet you at the Windmill Bastion.'

The phone clicked; she was gone. Frustrated, Eric stared angrily at the phone. She'd rung off before he was able to tell her he had no intention of driving up to Berwick without more information than the fact she thought she needed him.

He banged the receiver down. What the hell was this all about?

Then he was struck by a sudden thought. He rang reception. 'Has Mr Reynolds left yet?'

'He's just going out of the door, Mr Ward. Do you want him?'

'Yes,' Eric said swiftly. 'I'm coming right down.'

He hurried from the room and down the stairs. Reynolds was standing just inside the main door to the street. He seemed to have recovered his composure now. 'You wanted me, Mr Ward?'

Eric nodded, then hesitated. 'You . . . er . . . you knew Harry Staughton, and you came across Greg Bowles also, didn't you?'

'That's right. In Singapore. When we did the deal on the *Arctic Queen* between Artaros and Malaysia Mobile.'

'Did you . . . did you ever meet someone called Leah Bowles?'

Les Reynolds stared at Eric; his gaze was almost owlish. 'Well, yes, of course I knew her. Got to know her quite well. We were quite friendly . . . me, and Harry Staughton and Leah. We had a few drinks and laughs together. Why do you ask?'

Eric hesitated, then shook his head, frowning. 'It doesn't matter.'

He turned away, to return upstairs. Les Reynolds remained near the doorway, staring at him. He called after him, suddenly.

Eric turned. 'Yes?'

'I've just realized,' Les Reynolds said slowly, and shook his head.' You didn't know, Mr Ward, did you? You hadn't heard.'

'Know? Heard what?'

Reynolds shuffled, awkwardly. 'About Leah. And Harry.'

'For God's sake, what about them?'

But even as he said it, Eric knew. There had been a

woman at the villa with Harry Staughton when he died.

'Didn't you know?' Reynolds asked wonderingly. 'Didn't anyone ever *tell* you that Harry Staughton ran off from Singapore with Greg Bowles's missus?'

CHAPTER 5

1

Since the A1 had bypassed the town it had been relieved of the worst of its traffic, so the cascade of narrow grey streets with their Dutch-tiled roofs was now quieter and less congested. The town centre itself was busy enough, and Marygate was crowded with late afternoon shoppers, but as he walked into Scotsgate there were fewer people, which was probably what Leah Bowles had wanted.

She had been edgy and scared on the phone. Now that he knew she had been Harry Staughton's mistress, and had probably been with him when he was murdered, he could understand why her voice had been breathy and nervous when she spoke to him.

A friend had recommended him.

Eric was puzzled by the recommendation. He couldn't think who the link might be: it wasn't important, however, and he would probably find out from her, but it niggled at him. In the circumstances, he could hardly imagine it would have been Greg Bowles, the husband she had run away from to be with Harry Staughton.

She was a very careful, scared woman.

And she insisted that he had to come to her. It meant he had a long drive north to Berwick.

At least she had given him time to sort out his business at the office. He cleared his desk, went back to the flat he and Anne maintained in Gosforth and rang her to explain he'd be coming home the following evening, since he would be driving further north next day.

The rendezvous had been chosen with care. Windmill Bastion was a fairly isolated spot on the old city walls, overlooking the sea. Eric left the car near the Royal Tweed Bridge and walked into Marygate, through Scotsgate and climbed the steps on to the massive city walls that encircled the ancient town, the scene of many battles for supremacy between the Scots and the English. He walked eastwards to the Cumberland Bastion; he stood beside the old cannon and looked around.

There were a few children playing on the walls, and some men down on the beach poaching salmon with nets—an activity the police seemed to ignore in Berwick. Normally, there was a fine view of the Farne Islands from these walls but a curtain of grey mist hung offshore, blotting out Bamburgh and Holy Island.

Eric walked slowly along until he came to Ravensdowne Barracks and then stepped over the iron tracks and old gun emplacements to climb up to Windmill Bastion. He stood there for several minutes, looking down on the children's playground below him, complete with its climbing frame built in the shape of a military tank.

'Mr Ward?'

Eric turned, startled. She had come up behind him softly, from where she had been hidden by the wall. She presented a nondescript appearance: a muffled figure in a man's tweed overcoat, collar turned up against the gusting breeze here on the bastion, a woollen cap pulled down over her ears.

'Mrs Bowles?'

She nodded nervously and glanced around, checking that he was alone, with no one lurking in the near vicinity. 'Do you know the Lions' House?'

Eric nodded. Down below the disused magazine house there was an old building guarded by two stone lions. It was now split into three flats. 'Are you staying there?' he asked.

'No. Turn down the path by way of Brown's Hotel. You'll find a row of eighteenth-century cottages. It's number thirty-five. I'll be there—but don't follow me now. Give me three minutes.'

Before he could respond she had turned and was hurrying down past the magazine house. Eric was irritated: her cloak and dagger manner was surely overdoing things somewhat. There was no one around, apart from a big man in a dark windcheater at the far end of the wall, staring out to sea, bird-watching with a pair of powerful binoculars. Eric checked his watch. Three minutes. What the hell was all this about?

When the time was up he walked quickly down towards the Lions' House. He found the grey stone cottages and the No. 35 she had mentioned easily enough. He knocked on the door. It remained closed to him. He knocked again.

He heard a window closing upstairs, probably where she had been peering out to check if he had been followed. There was the sound of feet on a staircase. The door opened and she let him in.

She led the way down a stone-flagged passageway into a small Victorian sitting-room: the fireplace was cast iron with inlaid coloured tiles; a grandfather clock stood in the corner beside a Welsh dresser; the chairs were deep, heavily brocaded, the thick carpet dusty, and the wallpaper was dark, stained with age. There was the odour of dampness and disuse about the place.

She stood facing him. Her hair was long and dark, her eyes blue and scared. There was a recent, reddish scar on her temple. She wore a high-necked sweater and jeans: she was tall, long-legged, with a skin that had been tanned, but the tan was fading. She wore no make-up, and any pretence she might have had to emphasize the attractive bone structure of her face had now gone. She was a very frightened woman.

'Thank you for coming,' she said breathlessly. Her voice was deep, and shaky.

'How can I help you?' Eric asked quietly, without preliminaries.

'I need protection.'

'The police—'

'No. Not yet. I need protection . . . somewhere safe to hide.'

'I don't understand. I don't know what your problem is, though I imagine it's something to do with the death of Harry Staughton.' He paused, noted the way she flinched. He went on, 'The police could surely look after you, if you tell them—'

'No. He killed Harry, and he'll kill me. And he can buy people. That's why I got to be somewhere safe, before I can talk to the police. This was my grandmother's house, he never knew about it, but he could find me here, he can buy information. I'm scared, Mr Ward, and I need someone I can trust.'

'You have friends?'

'Yes, but no one I can be certain of. He knows about them . . . he could get to me through them. A stranger is better . . . someone uninvolved, someone I can trust.'

'You've already been in touch with someone.'

'What?' she asked, startled.

'The person who recommended me.'

'Oh—yes, of course, but I didn't even dare give away this address. He offered to help, but I didn't dare. You don't understand. If it's anyone he knows, he could inveigle—'

'Who was it recommended me?'

'What?' She stared at him uncomprehendingly, and then she brushed the question aside with an impatient wave of her hand. 'It doesn't matter. The fact is, I must get away from here. I feel unsafe here. I've been here too long, he might discover the address . . .'

'Now wait a minute.' Eric held up a hand. 'We're going around in circles. I'm getting confused. Let's get a few things straight, first of all. You were with Harry Staughton when he died?'

'Yes.'

'You know who killed him?'

She nodded, and shuddered.

'Did you see the killer, then?'

'I saw him . . . and more.'

'Who was it?'

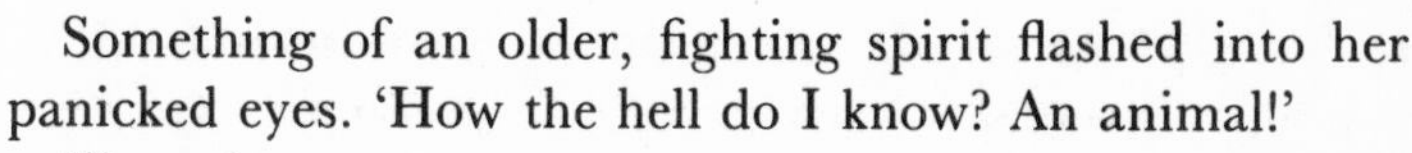

Something of an older, fighting spirit flashed into her panicked eyes. 'How the hell do I know? An animal!'

'But—'

'I know who sent him, that's the important thing,' she said venomously. 'It's because I ran away—I went with Harry. Now he's killed Harry, and he'll kill me if he finds me. He'll send that monster again—'

'Who are you talking about?'

'Who the hell else? My husband, of course! *Greg Bowles!*'

The words suddenly poured out in a torrent.

She was hurting. There was blood on the inside of her thighs and every muscle in her lower body ached. Dazed, she turned over on her side and the cold marble of the floor was hard under her bruised hip, where he had thrown her violently into the hallway.

Her head was throbbing, her lower stomach felt as though it had been ripped open, and as she got to her knees she felt a wave of sick revulsion flooding over her as she remembered how it had been, the violence, the pounding, the harsh, contemptuous breathing in her face as he had thrust at her. There was a bitter taste in her swollen mouth, and one of her teeth was loose. He hadn't been satisfied with raping her, he had needed to humiliate her, make her do things which made her stomach turn . . .

There were voices in the sitting-room. She had only a vague recollection of Harry coming back. He had finished by then; the animal had been standing by the window when Harry came back, and he had thrown her into the hallway when Harry came into the house through the rear entrance. She had wanted to call, she had opened her mouth to warn

Harry but the big man had hit her, a glancing blow that had ripped open her temple and sent her half stunned to the floor. It seemed long, long hours earlier . . .

She could hear Harry's voice.

He was arguing, pleading in a passionate tone. It would do him no good . . . not with that animal.

She couldn't rise from her knees. With her torn dress trailing, she began to crawl across the marble floor, whimpering lightly, dragging herself towards the rear entrance. Something was thrown down violently in the sitting-room behind her, perhaps the bookcase overturning, the crash of the music centre, shattering glass. She had reached the kitchen; she hauled herself to her feet at the kitchen table. The door at the back was unlocked. She opened it, and lurched outside.

The night was clear and starlit and warm. A soft cool breeze touched her cheek, rustling through the oleander hedge and bringing the scent of pine and rosemary to her nostrils. The pool shone and glittered under the starlight across to her left. She began to stagger, then moved slowly, carefully, down along the grass beside the drive, walking away from the house, away from the violence and the hurt and the danger.

She was near the gates when she heard the gunshot, and the silence swept in, throbbing in her head.

Harry was dead.

She knew it. In a matter of moments the animal would go into the hallway and realize she had gone. He would come after her: he could not afford to let her live, if he had killed Harry.

The thought gave her strength, pumped adrenalin into her veins, pushed her aching muscles up the slope and into the scrubland that surrounded the house. The roadway was useless: he would find her in minutes if she struck out for the village, five miles away. And she lacked the strength to struggle far. She must move away from the house, under the trees, through the maquis and the sharp spines of the scrub palm bushes, scrabble through the painful undergrowth until she could find a place to lie down and wait, or die.

Her legs were torn, sharp pains in her calves and thighs, but there was a sharpness in her lower stomach too, where he had hurt her, deliberately, viciously. She was panting and crying as she struggled on, but it was a slow process, painful, and the breath grew laboured in her chest as she struggled near the top of the crest. The trees were around her, tall ghostly pines outlined against the starlight. The ground was rocky, sharp limestone crags tearing at her. She fell. She lay still. The minutes passed.

She heard him.

He was a beast, and he moved like one. He came softly, gently, almost whispering through the trees. The light sound of his passage was menacing, the slow murmuring movement of approaching death. She moaned, deep in her throat, and began to drag herself up towards the crest. The rock and the spines tore at her knees and hands but she was reaching the top of the slope. There was the glitter of the sea ahead of her, a dark expanse marked with sparkling lights, dancing on the surf she could hear vaguely in her throbbing head. The stones under her were sharp-toothed and her hands and knees were sore and bleeding. She pulled herself forward and put out her hand, to grasp air. For a moment she was poised, and then she fell forward as the stone tilted. She crashed into the spiny bushes and rolled, and something hard hit her in the ribs. She gasped, breathless, and lay still.

Behind her the hill was silent.

When she regained her breath she tried to focus on her surroundings. She was lying at the foot of a straggly pine tree, among thick bushes. Above her she could see the rocky outcrop from which she had fallen; it shadowed her and the foot of the tree. She had no strength to go on. She stayed still, and tried to fight against the panic that was loud in her throat. Her breathing slowed, and the dimness came again, spreading a grey mist over her eyes. She lapsed into half-consciousness, aware only of the slow throbbing of pain that beat dully at her whole body. The minutes passed, slowly, and the haziness drifted over her against the slow background throbbing of the sea against the cliffs far below.

He cleared his throat, lightly.

She had no idea how long she had been lying there, half-conscious, but the harsh, grating sound brought her back to startled wakefulness. She remained still, hidden by the bushes but as she looked up to the rocky promontory she could see him, tall, black, menacingly outlined against the stars. He stood with his head thrown back, listening, his thick, overlong hair lifting in the breeze. She remembered the greasy touch of it as it had swung into her face, the fetid odour of his breath . . .

He stood there, and he turned his head slowly, and he looked down, directly towards where she lay.

She was frozen, panic-stricken. He stared at her for a long time, and she thought he was playing a cat and mouse game with her, until she almost screamed at him to come down and finish it, but as the seconds passed she realized he could not see her. The darkness of the shadowed base of the pine concealed her: he was waiting, listening, concentrating . . . and she was rigid with fear.

His head came up suddenly, the starlight glinting on the gun in his hand. He turned his head, his attention caught by a nocturnal movement among the trees.

Then he was gone, swiftly and silently.

She made no movement.

The night lengthened and she slept for a while, weariness overcoming her panic. She heard the gulls and she opened her eyes and the light came, tipping the pines with green and red, but still she lay where she had fallen. She dozed again through the long morning. Flies buzzed on the dried blood on the inside of her thighs and fussed busily over the wounds on her legs and arms and hands. Her head was throbbing, a rhythmic, dull ache that kept her drowsy. It was mid-afternoon before she moved, and the sun was hot on her face as she slowly climbed back up to the promontory, stiff, sore and aching in every part of her body.

The villa lay below her, normal; the pool glittered blue, the awnings fluttering gaily in the light breeze that always touched the house, maintaining a coolness in even the hottest weather. She had been happy there, with Harry. She sat down, and stared, and waited, and at last, in the late afternoon, she went back down to the house.

'You went back to the villa?' Eric asked incredulously. 'That was taking a hell of a chance!'

She shook her head. 'What else was I to do? The state I was in—and anyway, was it so much a chance, really? I worked it out. That man—that animal, he couldn't afford to wait around. He didn't know where I was. There was the chance I'd got away, was raising the alarm. He didn't dare hang around too long. So I waited, and when I thought it was safe, I went back.'

'What happened then?'

Leah Bowles was silent for a few minutes. 'It was a mess. The place had been wrecked. But Harry wasn't there. He'd gone; there was no sign of him. But I'd heard a shot—and that man had come to kill Harry. I'd got in the way. He'd used me to while away the time till Harry returned. Harry and I . . . we'd had an argument, you see, at the restaurant. Anyway, I took a shower, as much as anything to get rid of the smell of him. I attended to the cuts, cleaned myself up, got dressed. I had some money, got my passport—'

'You didn't phone for the police?' Eric asked.

'I tried. The phone lines had been cut. And later, I thought better of it, anyway. I needed to get out of Spain, get back somewhere familiar, where I could hide from Greg. He never liked losing, you know—and it wouldn't be enough just to kill Harry.'

Eric stared at her. 'Are you *seriously* suggesting it was your husband who killed Staughton?'

Her eyes were dark with a vicious hate. 'You don't know him like I do. It was never about love—it was about possession. I was a chattel, that's all—decorative, something he could show off. Once or twice, he even intimated I should be . . . nice to businessmen he was working with. But while he would have accepted that—using his chattel—it was another matter for me to leave him.'

'Did you tell him you were leaving?'

'I didn't dare. He would have been infuriated. That's why, I told Harry, if we were to go, it had to be well away, and under a different name, or he'd find us.'

'Even so, to set out to kill—'

'Oh, he wouldn't be involved, not personally, of course,' she said bitterly. 'But he hired that animal to do it for him. My best bet after that was to get back to England. Where Greg Bowles couldn't find me.'

Eric thought back to the occasions when he had met Greg Bowles. A cold, angry man—and one who had certainly been interested in the whereabouts of Harry Staughton. He had tried to find out how much Eric knew. The reason was now clear.

'Will you help me?' Leah Bowles asked desperately.

She didn't know that he had a business connection with Greg Bowles over the Iberica bid. Perhaps he should tell her . . . On the other hand, it made no difference, there was no conflict of interest, and if he told her she'd be panic-stricken.

'Please, Mr Ward, you must help me.'

'Yes. Don't worry. I'll do what I can.' Eric considered the matter for a little while. Leah Bowles was scared and excited, but there was the ring of conviction in her words. He still thought it would be better to go to the police, but if he were to suggest it she could become hysterical. Her story was wild, and he needed to check it out further with her, but there could be no harm in doing as she asked.

'All right.' He nodded. 'I think I know of a place. My

wife and I live at Sedleigh Hall, near the Cheviot. There's an old lodge on the estate—we use it occasionally as a guest house. I could take you there. You'd be safe . . . we could talk further.'

'I want revenge,' she said sharply.

Eric hesitated. 'We'll talk about it when I get you to Sedleigh.'

'Not just for killing Harry.' Her eyes were blazing in her cold face. 'It's for what was done to me, too.'

Eric stared at her, feeling the rage and the hurt and the anger seeping through. He nodded. 'All right. Come on, get your things together. I'll take you back south.'

'No.'

Eric looked at her, surprised. 'I thought—'

'Your car might be recognized. You might have been followed.'

'I think it hardly likely,' Eric protested.

'But it's possible,' she insisted. 'They'd know your car. It's better if I make my own way there. I need a hire car—and directions.'

He shrugged. 'If you wish. Hiring a car is no problem. I'll ring—'

'No.' She was staring at the phone on the sideboard as though it were suddenly lethal. 'Go out—get me a car. Get them to leave it beyond the post office, at the top end of the town, near the Buttermarket.'

'Your phone is ex-directory, Mrs Bowles.'

She stared at it in a fascinated horror. 'I've used it too much. I called friends. I called you. They could trace it back here. I've used it too much.'

She was shaking. Eric thought she was being unreasonable: the likelihood of the calls having been traced by Greg Bowles or anyone else was remote, and she was overreacting. But her fear was real, nevertheless. He decided it was best to humour her. He sat down, found a sheet of paper and scribbled some directions. 'All right. This will get you to the lodge. It'll take you about an hour or so to drive there. I'll arrange a car for you. Wait here for me.'

She made no reply.

He left quickly. He walked back into Marygate and found a car hire office. They were fully booked, but were able to advise him of another car rental business near Berwick Bridge. He made his way there hurriedly, walking to Bridge End and past Berwick Castle, now the site of the railway station. He found the rental office and arranged for the hire of a small Ford. They were satisfied when he produced his credit card but there was a little delay while the car was made ready.

Dusk had fallen by the time he drove out, past Bridge End and back into the town. He decided to leave the car where she had suggested, near the Buttermarket, though it seemed to him another example of her overcautious attitude. He locked the car and walked back to Leah Bowles's house. Infected by her anxiety now, he checked from time to time, to see if he was being followed.

It seemed not.

Even so, at the top of Scotgate he doubled back on himself, hurrying through the emptying streets, and cutting down through a narrow, echoing alleyway that brought him back into Marygate.

There was no sign of pursuit.

He cursed under his breath. He was vaguely angry with himself. He was overreacting, as Leah Bowles was overreacting. The lights were coming on in the streets as he walked down towards the old cottages. A cold wind had risen, lifting the hair at the back of his neck.

He reached No. 35 and it was in darkness. She was a frightened woman: she wouldn't wish to announce her presence in the house. He tapped lightly on the door.

It swung open at his touch.

Alarmed, he stepped inside. There were no lights on in the narrow passageway and broken glass crunched under his feet on the stone flags. He walked quickly forward, one hand on the stone wall for guidance in the darkness. The door to the sitting-room was closed, but no light shone through in the space under the door.

'Mrs Bowles?'

His voice echoed emptily in the passageway. He walked forward, hand outstretched. He pushed open the door to the sitting-room and stopped.

There was no sound in the house until, incongruously, the grandfather clock suddenly chimed, one sonorous, important note. It echoed eerily in the passageway, and up the stairs behind him.

'Mrs Bowles?'

Hesitantly, he took one step forward, and it was like that time long ago in an alleyway off Northumberland Street in Newcastle. He heard the brief rustling sound, the swish of the blow and he dived forward, instinctively, as he had dived in that alleyway years ago.

The blow took him on the shoulder, numbing the muscle in his neck as he went crashing forward. He went down, rolling forward, hurtling into the Welsh dresser and hearing plates and cups smashing around him as he careered into the fireplace.

He felt something soft under his hand, wet and yielding, a warm stickiness on his fingers, and then he turned, struggling upright as his attacker came in with a rush. Something sliced across Eric's upper arm and he knew he was fighting for his life.

2

In seconds the room was a shambles. The force of the man's rush sent Eric sprawling backwards to crash into the old grandfather clock. It came hammering down upon them with a jangling, splitting sound and glass showered over them as they struggled, their feet stamping in the dusty carpet. In the collapse of the heavy clock, however, Eric's assailant seemed to have lost the knife, and he was scrabbling for Eric's throat. A moment later, fingers dug deep, into Eric's windpipe.

It was a long time since he had been on a training programme for this kind of rough-house. He'd been told then, however, and the words came back to him now: keep control, don't panic, or you're lost.

He attempted to prise the grip free, but it was fierce. He was aware of the man's knee probing for his groin, and he swung his thigh sideways in protection. He bent slightly at the knees, slipped his arms inside the killer's grip and with a sudden surge thrust upwards, breaking the man's stiffened arms outward so the grip on Eric's throat was lost.

There was no respite.

The man came in again swiftly, flailing with his fist, seeking to hammer his forearm into Eric's neck. Eric cannoned backwards again, stumbling over the wreck of the grandfather clock in the darkened room, and as his assailant came in he kicked out, felt the toe of his shoe strike bone just below his assailant's kneecap, and then there was a sudden pause, when the two men stood facing each other in the darkness, harsh breath rasping in the silence.

Eric's eyes were getting used to the dimness in the room. The man facing him was big, broad-shouldered. His hair was almost shoulder length. But there was no time to think as with a sudden movement his opponent grabbed one of the easy chairs and heaved it, sliding it in Eric's direction, knocking him off balance.

For a moment he teetered crazily, aware that if he went down there was the chance he would never get up. But the big man was diving for him again, crashing into him, and he went down, and this time the man was heavy on him, pinning him to the dusty carpet, forearm pressed against Eric's windpipe, fingers clawing at Eric's face, seeking his eyes.

Desperately Eric twisted his head away, trying to pummel at the man's face, but his brain was beginning to fog, his senses leaving him as the pressure on his windpipe increased. He could feel himself slipping away, a red mist rising before his eyes, and he hammered at his assailant's head but the man was too close, his breath fetid in Eric's nostrils.

Eric rocked, supporting himself with his hands as he tried to unbalance the man on top of him. His fingers dug into the carpet and then there was something hard beneath his hand as he flailed about in his agony.

It took all of five seconds for it to register. It was the knife. Eric scrabbled in the carpet again as the red mist grew thick, and then the blade was under his hand. His fingers closed over the haft of the weapon, he lifted it and drove the point at the man's arm.

There was a grunt of pain, a weakening of the pressure. Eric thrust at the man's arm again, and the pressure was suddenly off, his assailant rolling sideways to escape the blade. Coughing in the dust rising from the carpet, Eric struggled up, lurching to his knees, the knife still in his grip and the man facing him was growling, deep in his throat. Eric stood up slowly; his opponent facing him was uncertain, wary, backing away. There was a long silence, broken only by the harsh, laboured breathing of the two men.

Then the second easy chair came sliding across the carpet, tumbling in Eric's direction. Eric avoided it, and stepped forward, but the door crashed open, and was violently banged shut again. Footsteps echoed, running in the stone-flagged passageway.

Eric made no attempt to follow. He was exhausted; his head was throbbing, his throat dry, and there was a dull ache in his shoulder where the knife had first sliced him.

He dropped to his knees again in the dark room. He stayed like that for a little while, the breath rasping in his chest, his throat sore and aching. Then slowly he leaned forward, crawling towards the fireplace, his hand extended.

Leah Bowles was lying there, unmoving, among the wreckage of the room. He groped forward to her dark shape and his hand struck her leg, her thigh. He moved upwards, to her waist; her jeans were torn, her sweater ripped and he felt the wetness and knew the blood was seeping stickily from her stomach.

His fingers sought the pulse in her throat.

There was none.

'So we meet again,' Detective-Inspector Tony O'Connor said pleasantly enough as he sat down heavily on the hospital chair beside Eric. 'I preferred the previous locale.'

'The beer isn't as good here,' Eric admitted. 'But they do stop the bleeding.'

'How is it?'

Eric grimaced at his arm. 'Not deep, really. Bit of a slice, more than anything else. I've had worse, in the old days. It's my throat bothers me more. Sore as hell.'

'Looks like he wanted to turn your lights out.'

'I got that impression,' Eric replied.

'Why?'

Eric shrugged. He looked out of the window of the hospital room to which the ambulance had rushed him after he had phoned. The lights of the town were on now, illuminating the streets, shining on the castle and the rail bridge out of Berwick, running south. 'I don't know. My guess is I came back a bit too soon. He was after her. She was afraid he would find her. It seems she was right. But me . . . I can't think of any reason why he should want to kill me, particularly.'

'Shakespeare suggested killing all the lawyers.'

'And all coppers are bastards,' Eric countered.

O'Connor laughed, a short, barking sound. 'So if it wasn't a lawyer-hater, who was it? Didn't you get a look at him?'

'No. The room was dark. He was big, and he had long hair. That's all I could give you.'

'Not much, for an experienced ex-copper. We might get his prints, of course, but with you handling the knife as well, could be you'll have destroyed them. Didn't think of that, did you?'

'I had other things on my mind—like self-preservation.'

O'Connor paused. 'So who was the woman?'

'A client.'

'With a deep stomach wound. He'd twisted the knife. It would have hurt. There was a wound to the throat too, but it looks to me that wasn't the one that killed her. Maybe in the struggle . . . No, he killed her, and enjoyed hurting her as he did it. Not a nice man, this guy. But you said she told you he was looking for her. You haven't told me who she was.'

Eric caressed his sore throat. 'Her name was Leah Bowles. She'd asked me to come to see her at Berwick. She wanted protection.'

'From the guy who killed her?'

'From her husband.'

'That was her *husband*?' O'Connor asked, astonished.

Eric shook his head. 'No. But she was afraid her husband would send someone after her. Maybe he did. I don't know.'

'Do you know the guy she was married to?'

'I've come across him.'

Tony O'Connor stared at Eric for several seconds. He nodded. 'All right, I'd better hear what this is all about. Talk to the man, bonny lad.'

The reception Eric received at Sedleigh Hall was mixed. He had phoned in advance, so that Anne was prepared, but when he finally arrived she welcomed him passionately, in relief, and then veered towards upbraiding him for insisting on working in such a dangerous business. He'd heard it all before, and his head was aching, but she was quite right, of course. Working as a corporate lawyer for Morcomb Enterprises was bound to be a safer occupation than this.

He made no response, however, and after a while she calmed down. He was aware it was the tension and anxiety that had got to her. When he showed her the superficial nature of the wound and assured her that he was quite all right, her natural curiosity got the better of her and she asked him for the full story. He told her as much as he was able.

'You've no idea who this man might be—the one who attacked you?'

Eric shook his head. 'I don't. It seems she didn't know, either. But . . . well, the way he killed her, the pleasure he took in hurting her . . . I mean, he could have cut her throat and she would have died more quickly. The man who killed Harry Staughton in Spain . . . she described him as an animal, several times. I think it was the same man. He'd missed her in Spain; he caught up with her in Berwick.'

'And she says Greg Bowles ordered it?'

Eric sighed. 'I only discovered recently that Leah Bowles had run off with Harry Staughton. When Staughton was killed, she was convinced it was Bowles getting his revenge. That was why she was so scared.'

'She had reason to be!'

'Yes, but she had seen the killer. It could be he was after her, not because he was under orders, but because she could identify him.'

Anne rose and walked across the room to pour each of them a stiff drink. She sat down beside him on the settee again.

'But she thought she was in a safe house. How did this man find her?'

Eric shook his head. 'I don't know. She'd used the phone, but it was ex-directory. She told me she'd rung friends, presumably to tell them she was all right. She didn't identify them. One of them had recommended me to her.'

'Who was it?

'I don't know.'

'And why you?'

Eric shrugged. 'Again, I don't know. She really just wanted a stranger, someone she could trust because he wasn't involved, and wasn't known to her husband. She was afraid her friends in England might somehow betray her whereabouts to her husband.'

'So how did he find out where she was?'

'If it *was* him,' Eric said carefully. 'I haven't the faintest idea. She herself was scared that her husband would use his money to trace her—she was terrified of the possibility.'

There was another possibility, of course. The killer had found Leah Bowles by following Eric north. It was a thought he did not wish to dwell upon.

Eric stayed at Sedleigh Hall for the next few days and rested. There were no calls, and he wondered whether Anne was protecting him. He made no complaint. He began to chafe, nevertheless, at the enforced inactivity by the following weekend, and went riding with Anne. Having come through that ordeal unscathed—he did not share Anne's passion for horse-riding—he announced he'd get back to the Quayside office on Monday. Anne raised objections, but they were half-hearted: she could see how restless he was.

There were various messages waiting for him, and a sheaf of papers on the progress of the Iberica bid. It seemed that the publicity given to Matt Coleman in the Cooper article had halted for a period the flow of investors prepared to sell to the arbitrageur. The impact had not been decisive, however, and Iberica had issued another press statement, Coleman denying the charges made in the Cooper article and railing against 'financial gutter journalism'. The result had been a tremor in the market-place, and a slow bleeding away again, of stockholders defecting to pick up the high prices now dominating the Artaros stock.

The matter still hung in the balance.

Leonard Channing rang on Tuesday morning. 'Eric, where the hell have you been? I rang your office—I rang Sedleigh Hall, and Anne said you were unavailable.'

'She's protective. I've had some problems.'

'Well, tell her she's being over-protective! The Iberica bid is *your* affair—the board's left it in your hands. I've no intention of stepping in at this crucial stage, but there's something odd going on. Greg Bowles is also unavailable, and his aides have been around here. They wanted to see you. They have a package addressed to you. It's marked confidential. What do you want me to do with it?'

His curiosity would be burning him. Eric smiled grimly. 'Send it up by special delivery. To my office at the Quayside.'

'I could—'

'Just send it, Leonard.'

It was waiting for him when he arrived at the office next morning.

The package contained a sheaf of documents, some photocopied transcripts of court proceedings, and a selection of official company files stamped with the mark of the Securities and Exchange Commission. Some newspaper cuttings were attached and a summary sheet signed by one of Bowles's aides. There was also a letter, signed by Greg Bowles.

It was brief, and to the point.

Dear Mr Ward

It would seem your thoughts about North Lagoon were apposite. You'll find enclosed the relevant documents. In addition, there is a summary of their contents. We trust you will take the necessary action.

Eric turned to the summary sheet.

SUMMARY: CORPORATE RAID FUNDING

1. North Lagoon, Inc. is a publicly quoted company in Virginia. It is an investment company, which specializes in the handling of pension fund accounts. Its stock is held by three other companies: Edeltel; Mack Securities; Plaza Enterprises. Control of the last two of these companies

lies in the hands of Matt Coleman: altogether, through these holdings he can be said to hold a controlling interest to the extent of sixty per cent in North Lagoon, Inc. itself.

2. There are cross-holding arrangements between North Lagoon, Inc. and the following major companies: Centre Microchip; Stanhouse Stores; Golden House Engineering. Matt Coleman holds trusteeships in each of these companies.

3. According to SEC records, the following corporate raids were made by Coleman during the period 1985–90: Telsky; Transatlantic; Freiburg Telecommunications; Atkins Securities; Bushnell Airways; Mackenzie Stores.

4. Company records demonstrate that pension fund monies of the companies mentioned in 2 above, and of North Lagoon itself, were drawn upon to fund the raids in each of the operations mentioned in 3 above, with the exception of Bushnell Airways which was funded by a junk bond issue.

5. North Lagoon, Inc. receives thirty per cent of any profit accruing to the pension funds under its management, in addition to normal broking fees. Coleman thus benefits indirectly from the publicly quoted companies of which he is chairman or director. It is calculated from the records that more than $85m has been channelled through North Lagoon during the period on inquiry.

Conclusion
The activity noted above appears to be in breach of US law, which prohibits pension fund money being used for the benefit of a company trustee, director or major shareholder.

Eric leaned back in his chair and pursed his lips thoughtfully. It looked as though the Iberica bid was about to founder with all hands. Once the details of the operations ferreted out by the Artaros aides were made public, confidence in the market-place would evaporate, there would be a rush to flee from Iberica, the share price of Artaros would dip and the crisis would be over.

Carefully, Eric went through the supporting documentation. It took him well over two hours before he was satisfied that the information in the papers supported the general conclusions noted in the summary sheet. The main thing now was to ensure that the news hit the streets before Iberica, and Matt Coleman, got wind of it. Once it was made public, the Iberica bid would collapse.

Eric looked at the summary again. He had no doubt that once the raid had been fought off, the details would be forwarded to the Securities and Exchange Commission. Matt Coleman might have hoped to escape the clutches of the SEC by coming to Europe, but with this information, they would quickly drag him back. And if they did, his European venture could be over, almost before it started.

He rang his secretary.

'Yes, Mr Ward?'

'Will you get me Phil Cooper, please, in London?'

During the next few days matters moved quickly. Phil Cooper's article sent a tremor through the financial press; there were leaders in all the broadsheets, and the tabloids screamed fraud. Matt Coleman came out with a series of statements which denied the truth of the items mentioned in Cooper's article, and suggested that Bowles was fighting a smear campaign unprecedented in the annals of financial journalism. Phil Cooper countered two days later with quotations from the SEC to the effect that they were calling for papers from a number of publicly quoted companies in the States in which Coleman was known, or suspected, to have an interest.

The managing director of Artaros was sought for his comments. He was unavailable. Three days later, the Iberica raid, which was now staggering and close to collapse, was wiped off the front pages by a sensational new item.

MD OF THREATENED COMPANY QUESTIONED ON MURDER CHARGE

Leonard Channing was quickly on the phone, fulminating about the damage Martin and Channing could suffer from being involved in business with a man charged with murdering his own wife.

'He's being *questioned*, Leonard, not charged.'

'It's all the same in the public mind. This could be very damaging, Eric.'

He implied that it was Eric's fault that they had got involved with Bowles and the Artaros bid in the first place, and Eric was certain that this would be the impression Channing would want to put to the board. The chairman of Martin and Channing was a past master at avoiding responsibility, as he was at gathering to himself undeserved plaudits.

Late in the week Eric received notification that the hearing into preliminary issues relating to *Malaysia Mobile v Ocean Distribution and International Charters* was put down for the following Thursday. It would be in chambers, before Master Simes David. He phoned Les Reynolds to warn him, and arranged a conference with Reynolds.

Tony O'Connor was in touch by phone the next morning.

'We're sending a car around this afternoon, bonny lad.'

'For me?'

'Who else? Got news. I told you we'd been chasin' a guy over credit card frauds. Got our hands on him at last. His name's Dave Mason: Soldier Mason, he's known as in the West End: a hard man. We're stickin' him in a line-up. We'd like you to take a look at him.'

'You think he's the man who killed Leah Bowles?'

'Mebbe so. But if you can't finger him, we got trouble. He's hard, like I said. We'll never get an admission out of him. But we'll see, hey? We'll have to wait and see.'

3

Business had brought Anne to Newcastle on Friday afternoon, so she was able to pick Eric up for the drive north: the bad news was that he had forgotten they had been invited to a wedding reception, held by an old schoolfriend of Anne's, at Cragside. They decided to leave it until Saturday morning to go north, and stayed at the Newcastle flat overnight.

It was a pleasant morning for the drive to Coquetdale. They left Newcastle mid-morning and headed for Alnwick, a fast drive along a reasonably quiet A1. From there they took the steeply climbing road out of the town to the open moor and Brizlee Wood, on the way to Rothbury. The air was clean, the sky an empty blue, and across to their right they could see the dark line of the Northumberland coast. Anne leaned her head back on the seat rest and sighed. She glanced at him quizzically.

'You've been pretty quiet about your experience at the line-up,' she said.

Eric grimaced, as he headed the car along the long, straight, rising road that gave a view of the Cheviots to the north-west.

'It wasn't exactly an uplifting experience.'

They had stood under the harsh light in the long narrow room, men of similar build, all dressed in dark clothing, windcheaters, jackets, long-haired, dark-visaged. O'Connor had taken Eric along the line, slowly: Eric had stared in the face of each man, but at the end of it all he had shaken his head. O'Connor, obviously disappointed, had told him to take his time, try again. Eric had done so, but he couldn't be sure. There was an image in his mind—the crouching, big man in the darkness—and there was a memory of a man with binoculars, standing on the bastion looking out to sea, birdwatching, when Eric had first met Leah Bowles. He had been big, dressed in a windcheater, but that was all Eric could remember.

And in all conscience, he could not have positively identified one man in the line-up.

'All you said last night was you couldn't pick him out. I know they always have to put in people of similar build and so on, but was there nothing you recognized?'

Eric shook his head. 'When I was attacked in that cottage, the room was dark. Of course, I gained impressions: the man was big, he had long hair, but I didn't make out his face.'

'There were no other characteristics you could pick out?'

'Such as what?' Eric asked, a trace of irritation entering his tone. 'You're sounding as critical as O'Connor. I wasn't in the business of looking at him carefully—I was too busy fighting him off.'

'But the man they've arrested—did he have a knife wound?' Anne persisted.

Eric nodded. 'This man Mason certainly has a wound in his upper arm. Apparently, he says he got it in a brawl in Morpeth. He declines to give details. All right, others in the line-up didn't have a wound, but the fact is there were no prints from Mason in the room, none they can identify, and I couldn't pick him out of the line. And the wound in itself isn't enough. To be big, and long-haired and carrying an arm wound might sound conclusive, knowing what we do, but it would get thrown out by the Crown Prosecution Service as being too weak. And I can't see any jury convicting on such a flimsy story, after they've been hectored by any counsel worth his salt.'

'You struggled with him. Wasn't there any other forensic evidence they could find?'

'Apparently not. I had a chat with O'Connor afterwards. They've done tests on his clothing—but of course, it's different clothing from that the killer wore in the attack. They've tested hair, fingernails, all the usual kind of thing, but they've come up with nothing. The labs at Gosforth are still working on it, of course, but from what O'Connor said, there's not much hope.'

'And this man Mason—he's let nothing slip?'

'Mason is just keeping his mouth shut—saying nothing, admitting nothing. But then, what's he got to lose? They can't pin this killing on him without more evidence. O'Connor tells me they're trying to confirm that Mason was in Spain at the time of Staughton's murder, through his use of stolen credit cards, but that'll be some time coming through. And there's nothing to fit him in at Berwick at the relevant time.' Eric shook his head. 'He's a hard man, apparently: he's done time before, and he's not afraid to do it again. A stretch for stealing credit cards doesn't bother him—murder would be another story. So why should he talk and incriminate himself? The chance of him breaking, and talking about Staughton and the rest of it, is unlikely.'

'He's not going to go free, surely?' Anne exploded.

'No, no . . . they've got him on the credit card charges, so he'll get some time inside for that. But whether prison will soften him up, so he talks about who hired him—if he *was* hired—is another matter.'

The road began to twist and turn, swinging past Corby's Crags, perched dramatically on the hillside, overlooking the disused Alnwick to Coldstream railway line. Eric was silent as they drove past the Edlingham Viaduct, and the castle and church. The rectory there had been the scene of a notorious armed robbery two centuries earlier: the two poachers sentenced to life imprisonment were released after ten years when others confessed, and the mistake had led to the creation of the Court of Criminal Appeal. Criminal investigations could go badly wrong, Eric thought, even when the police got their hands on the right man, unlike the Edlingham Rectory affair.

'Anyway,' he said, half to himself, 'I'm not too happy with the whole business of Staughton's murder.'

'You don't think Mason did it?' Anne asked in surprise.

'I don't mean that. He's a pretty strong candidate, it seems to me, for both murders, though it's another matter proving it. No, I'm just a bit leery about Leah Bowles's story.'

'You mean about her husband hiring this man to do the killing?'

Eric nodded. They crossed the A697 and the rich farmland was giving way to moorland and gorse. The road was climbing again until the crags of the Simonside Hills were outlined in the distance. 'You see,' he said slowly, 'Greg Bowles has been questioned, but O'Connor tells me they can't stick him with anything at the moment. He was out of the country when his wife was murdered, and they haven't as yet come up with any link between Mason and Bowles.'

'Leah Bowles was convinced her husband was responsible.'

'That's right. But she had a very personal view of the whole business, after all. She'd run away from Bowles—she'd be expecting trouble from him, knowing him the way she did. So it would be natural for her to assume Bowles was behind the killing of Staughton.'

'But she also was murdered. Doesn't that support her argument?'

'It could . . . But let's assume for a moment Bowles *didn't* order Mason to kill Leah. It could have been Mason's own idea, because she could identify him as the man who had murdered Staughton and raped her. That would put a different perspective on things, as far as Staughton's killing was concerned.'

'In what way?'

'Because as far as I can see, Bowles wasn't the only one who had a reason to kill Staughton. And if revenge wasn't the motive behind the murder of Staughton, others come into the frame.'

'Who else might want him dead?'

'There's Paul Lintern, of Ocean Distribution,' Eric suggested.

'You've not said much about him.'

'I met him in London. He's an angry, bitter man. He was conned by Harry Staughton. Ocean Distribution paid a sum of money to Staughton, who misappropriated it. I have a feeling Lintern has his board on the back of his neck: he didn't tell them as much as he should have done about his dealings with Staughton. He could be bitter enough to have wanted revenge on Staughton—and set up the killer.'

'Just because his company was defrauded? That sounds a bit thin to me,' Anne demurred.

'Well, maybe so,' Eric conceded. 'But I have an odd feeling about Lintern, and Reynolds and Staughton. It may well be that the whole story hasn't yet come out.'

'How do you mean?'

Eric grimaced. 'Look at it in the cold light of day. We've been told that Staughton was a charmer, a persuasive businessman who got people to like him—as he did Reynolds—but wasn't averse to defrauding them. But Paul Lintern is a businessman, a principal mover in a big company. He's no fool. And yet he claims he was taken in by Harry Staughton, hook, line and sinker. We end up with a charter agreement which Lintern is flourishing, and which Simon Chan claims doesn't represent the true agreement. That's what the case next week will be all about.'

'I don't see what you're driving at.'

Eric was silent for a few minutes. They were entering Rothbury Forest. In a quarter of a mile they would be turning into the driveway to Cragside, now owned by the National Trust but originally built by Lord Armstrong as a place to relax in. Eric drew in to the side, and parked in a small lay-by. He looked out over the hill, and the park drive that led to Tumbleton Lake. 'Let's put it like this,' he said, thinking aloud. 'We know that Harry Staughton skipped with a large amount of money. O'Connor tells me they still haven't traced the bank accounts—other than petty cash stuff Staughton kept in Spain. But when Staughton was murdered, the house was turned over. The guy who killed Staughton wasn't interested simply in killing him—he was looking for something.'

'Money?'

Eric shook his head. 'I doubt it. And if it wasn't money he was after, what was it he was trying to find?'

'If there *was* another motive for the killing, as you suggest,' Anne said slowly, 'that could let Greg Bowles off the hook.'

'Not necessarily,' Eric replied cautiously. 'We need to remember that Bowles had dealings with Staughton—the sale of the *Arctic Queen* by Artaros to Malaysia Mobile. It was during the period when Staughton first became friendly with Leah Bowles. What if there was something out of the ordinary about that deal? I mean, the signs on the surface are that Bowles managed to pull one over Staughton—sold him a ship that was getting weary in the timbers, so to speak. But doesn't that strike you as odd? Staughton was an experienced charter manager. Would he really buy something sub-standard, like the *Arctic Queen*, as simply as that?'

'I'm not clear—'

'What if there was something underhand about the deal? Some arrangement, between the parties . . .'

'Such as what?'

'I don't know,' Eric admitted grimly. 'It's just that I get an uneasy feeling about it all. You know what that cynic Ambrose Bierce says about commercial dealings: *A kind of transaction in which A plunders from B the goods of C and for compensation B picks the pocket of D of money belonging to E.* I wouldn't trust *any* of the characters involved in this whole business.' He shook his head thoughtfully. 'What if there were some documentation which would be embarrassing to Bowles, documentation held by Staughton? It could be a reason for killing him. After all, when Staughton skipped with his wife, what evidence do we have that Bowles seriously went after them?'

'You told me he showed some interest in your search for Staughton.'

'Well, yes, he was curious to know where Staughton was. But by then he might have known where the man was—and had already killed him through his hired gun!'

Anne remained silent for a little while, brooding. 'First you say it could be Bowles, then you say maybe not. You seem to me to be weaving cobwebs, theories without substance.'

Eric sighed. 'Maybe so. But it brings us back to Lintern. How come Staughton can make men like Bowles and Lintern seem gullible? What if there was more to it: whatever was in Staughton's villa, whatever documentation or anything else was being looked for—couldn't it perhaps have been incriminating as far as Lintern was concerned? Perhaps it was Lintern, not Bowles, who wanted the villa turned over! Maybe *he* sent the killer after Harry Staughton.'

'Under those kinds of scenario,' Anne scoffed, 'you could be pointing the finger at almost anyone who's ever been involved with Harry Staughton.'

'Precisely,' Eric agreed. 'Such as Simon Chan.'

The wedding reception was as noisy as wedding receptions usually were. Eric knew the bride, but not well, and the bridegroom was a stranger. Eric had a brief talk with him: he was an estate agent from Alnmouth, and inclined to talk of house prices and how poverty-stricken the profession was. Eric beat a retreat as soon as he decently could.

As the champagne flowed freely and the party grew more relaxed, Eric moved more to the fringes. From what he could see of Anne, she too was finding the occasion something of a strain. She knew a number of people there, but as with many childhood friendships, as people grew older they grew apart. She was no longer in touch with the kinds of lives most people there led: she was a businesswoman in her own right, with a large company to manage.

And her husband was considerably older than many in the room, Eric thought wryly.

She caught his eye, and came across to him, threading her way between the chattering groups. 'How you going?'

'I'm surviving.'

'I've had a word with the happy bride—told her we'll be leaving fairly soon. We'll have to wait a while, but I don't think anyone would object if we took a stroll in the garden; other young couples are doing it.'

Champagne glass in hand, Anne led the way out into the garden. They strolled in the late morning sunshine past the great clumps of rhododendron beyond the stables to the viewpoint above Tumbleton Lake and Nelly's Moss Lake. 'Did you know that Cragside was the first private house in the country to be fitted with electric light?' Anne asked.

'I did,' Eric replied solemnly.

'And were you serious about Simon Chan?'

Anne had that capacity for deer leaps of thought and conversation. Eric smiled. 'Well, let me put a few points to you—be my sounding-board.'

'Agreed.'

'Simon Chan came north to do a deal with Sir Henry Slocum.'

'Investigate the possibilities, at least.'

'Not quite the way Slocum saw it. However . . . Next, Chan approaches you, dangles the carrot of a possible deal with Morcomb Estates.'

'Correct.'

'But neither deal has materialized . . . and neither seems to be making progress.'

Anne waved her half-empty champagne glass in an expansive gesture, the businesswoman explaining things to her inexperienced husband. 'Well . . . yes . . . but Morcomb Estates are still hopeful. I don't know about Slocum, of course. These things do take time, Eric, and when you add the complication that we're dealing with a Chinese businessman—'

'But things aren't *happening*,' Eric insisted.

'No.' She paused, and looked at him with lowering brows. 'So what are you saying?'

Eric shrugged. 'Maybe Chan was in the North-East for a different reason. The appearance he gave was that he had come on business, and engaging me to find Staughton was . . . subsidiary. But what if it was the other way around?'

'How do you mean?'

'What if sniffing around the North-East for Staughton's traces was the *main* reason for his coming to Tyneside? What if the Slocum and Morcomb deals were just cover, providing him with an excuse to poke around up here for signs of his errant Vice President?'

'That's a bit far-fetched, Eric,' Anne protested.

'You say so, because you don't like to think you might be losing a deal,' Eric said, grinning at her. 'And, all right, maybe he *was* hoping to do business as well. But look at the facts. He engages me to look for Staughton. Once Staughton's dead, he drops me, and he doesn't come north again, the deals are in suspension, probably dying—'

'And Chan's gone to ground,' Anne said slowly. 'He's been *incommunicado* recently—we've tried contacting him, but his secretary is evasive.' She finished her champagne and glowered at Eric. 'You've clouded my morning. But what is it you're driving at?'

Eric leaned against a low stone wall and stared out across the trees to the hills above Rothbury. 'Just the thought that it could have been Chan who sent that killer to Spain.'

'But he was looking for Staughton here in the North-East!'

'Not so,' Eric corrected her. 'He engaged me to check on my contacts up here, to get a lead on Staughton's whereabouts. But I wasn't the only one involved. Chan admitted to me that he had a network of people, probably all trying to trace Staughton. And it is a powerful network. After all, when Staughton's body was found the first information was that his name was Suffolk. But Chan discovered his real identity before the newspapers did. In other words, he has friends in high places, speaking from the criminal investigation point of view. I was never central to his search for Harry Staughton—I was just a small additional cog. And once Staughton was dead, I was no longer of any use to Chan.'

'But he's such a *gentleman*!'

'Fu Manchu was a smiling Chinese villain,' Eric countered.

'You're not going to tell me Simon Chan wants to take over the world!'

Eric smiled. 'No. But I'm not so certain now that he told me the truth when he said he was under pressure from his Vice Chairman. That could have been just a story, to give him a credible reason for seeking Staughton—other than the real one, I think his real reason for looking for Staughton was pure revenge—he'd lost face, as well as money.'

'You really think he could have hired the killer?'

Eric shrugged. 'It's feasible. And now Staughton's paid for his actions with his life, Chan wants blood from Ocean Distribution and International Charters.'

'Will he get it, Eric?'

He looked at her, standing easily, with her hip against the wall, her light dress tightened against the long curve of her thigh, her left hand caressing the pendant between her breasts. The bright sunshine emphasized the reddish lights in her hair, made her wrinkle her nose as she narrowed her eyes against the brightness. She looked young, and desirable, the way she had looked in those early days when they had first met, up on the fell above Sedleigh Hall. She twirled the champagne glass in her right hand, and cocked her head on one side. '*So?*' she said, recognizing his change of mood.

Eric smiled. 'The answer to your first question is, we'll find out at the preliminary hearing next week. As to your second . . . I think we ought to take our leave of our hostess.

We'll be home within the hour, and I think I'd then like to curl up.'

'With a book?' she asked, moving closer to him and touching his mouth gently with slim, teasing fingers.

'I have a feeling,' he replied, 'there might be better alternatives on offer.'

CHAPTER 6

1

As a Master of the Supreme Court, Edward Simes David had developed a powerful reputation. His presence itself was formidable: he was a squat, heavy man, dark-skinned, bald apart from two springing tufts of coarse black hair above his ears, and his eyes were small, pale and piercing behind the heavy, horn-rimmed glasses he affected. It was rumoured he did not need the glasses for there was nothing wrong with his eyesight: they were worn for effect, for when he peered at a lawyer over the hornrims, legs turned to water. But apart from the power of his presence, he was known to be a direct man, and reckoned to be a fair one. His decisions were made swiftly; he was disinclined to prevaricate; he had a dry sense of humour; and he suffered no fools, time-wasting, or unreasonable behaviour.

'You will be aware, gentlemen, that as an officer of the Supreme Court I am in the position to exercise all the jurisdiction and powers, save a few exceptions, of a high court judge in chambers. This hearing before me in my chambers is to determine preliminary issues that may be dealt with before trial. I am also empowered to advise on the number of counsel that may be employed. That may affect the taxation of your case thereafter. In this hearing, while we may dispense with the normal rules of procedure that would apply in a court of law proper, I would wish, nevertheless, that you confine yourselves to matters in hand, be brief, and make no attempt to cloud issues.' He glowered at the assembled gruop over his hornrims. 'I abhor cloudy issues.'

There was silence in the room. The high mullioned windows let in long shafts of sunlight, in which dust particles danced. The polished table in front of Simes David gleamed; Eric glanced across the table to where Simon Chan sat impassively with two aides, staring at Master Simes David. Charles Davison sat beside Chan, confident, amused at the Master's peroration. At the other side of the table was Paul Lintern, whispering to a couple of his minions. His lawyer, a man called Evan Patrick, whom Eric knew vaguely, sat with folded arms, head lowered, staring at the papers in his lap.

'I also,' Master Simes David intoned, 'take it as my duty to persuade litigants not to be so foolish as to go to trial. If we can settle in chambers—everyone benefits. Especially the administration of the law.'

Eric wasn't so certain Charles Davison would agree: he'd be expecting a fat fee from Malaysia Mobile if this case could go to the High Court. Eric settled back as Davison was called upon to open.

He was good, there was no doubt about that. His delivery was smooth, his arguments concisely put, his manner controlled, respectful and elegant. It was impossible to determine what impression he made upon Simes David: the Master hunched forward in his chair, hands clasped over his chest, making a few notes from time to time, peering steadfastly at the man addressing him.

'So,' Davison was concluding, 'I might summarize the issues as these. My clients, Malaysia Mobile, entered into an agreement with Ocean Distribution, negotiated by the second defendant, International Charters. That agreement was relatively simple. The *Arctic Queen* was to be the subject of sale to Ocean Distribution. The price was agreed upon, and is the subject of no contention.'

He paused, shuffled some papers in front of him, and continued. 'There was one proviso attached to that sale. It related to a charter back agreement. The Charter Manager who arranged the sale signed an agreement which Malaysia Mobile accept as binding, and which, indeed, was acted upon: namely, that Malaysia Mobile would charter back, for a period of one year, the said *Arctic Queen* from Ocean Distribution. The charter was at the rate of £350,000 per month.'

He paused, as Simes David scribbled a note.

'The one-year charter was completed, to the satisfaction of both parties. The terms of the agreement had called for a first tranche of monies from Ocean Distribution, subject to the deduction of a sum for the first year charter, then payment of the remainder of the purchase price in due time. It is the contention of Malaysia Mobile that this balance is now due. Ocean Distribution are refusing to pay the balance. In essence, therefore, my clients demand payment of the full purchase price, and failing that, would wish to proceed with a suit claiming fraud and conspiracy on the part of the two defendants.'

Simes David grimaced and hunched further forward in his leather-backed chair. He grunted. 'So if the full purchase price is paid, the charges of fraud and conspiracy would be withdrawn?'

'The purchase price and costs,' Davison corrected.

Simes David scowled. 'We're talking generally of settlement here. Details can be dealt with later.' He peered over his glasses at Davison for a few moments after he sat down, then swung his heavy head towards Paul Lintern's lawyer. 'Response, Mr Patrick?'

The Ocean Distribution lawyer rose to his feet: thin, dark-suited, Evan Patrick had a reputation for being cold of manner and of disposition. 'Some admissions can be made, Master Simes David.'

'Let's have them.'

Patrick went through them quickly, covering the matter of the initial sale agreement, the negotiations between Les Reynolds, Lintern and Harry Staughton, and the purchase price for the *Arctic Queen*. 'Thereafter, my clients contend a significant issue has been denied by the plaintiffs. It is not that Ocean Distribution refuse to pay the full purchase price. It is that the plaintiffs are in breach of the agreement entered into.'

'You mean the charter?' Simes David inquired.

'Yes, Master. But not as stated. The agreement was to the effect that a charter of three years, not one, was the condition precedent to the sale. Malaysia Mobile now refuse to complete the further two years of the charter; so, consequently, they are in breach, and at trial my clients would vigorously defend their position and counterclaim for damages.'

'I'm certain they would,' Simes David growled drily. 'So . . . what we have here as an issue is the exact nature of the charter. Malaysia Mobile claim it was a one-year charter; Ocean Distribution argue it was a three-year charter. I have been supplied the necessary documentation. I am confused. They are contradictory. The plaintiff's copy of the agreement confirms *their* case: a one-year charter. The Ocean Distribution papers confirm a three-year charter. *Both* agreements are signed by Paul Lintern . . . and by J. H. Staughton, Charter Manager for Malaysia Mobile. But while the plaintiffs rely on the *one*, the first defendant relies on the *other*! I am at a loss here, gentlemen, to ascertain what on earth is going on.' He glowered at both lawyers, then fixed his glance on Eric. 'We have a second defendant, who seems to be the possible piggy in the middle. Mr Ward—do you wish to make a submission at this time?'

Eric rose. He was aware of Charles Davison watching him carefully: they had crossed swords before now and Davison was wary. 'Without wishing to speak for either side,' Eric said, 'and only in defence of my own client, Mr

Reynolds of International Charters, may I suggest the two issues which should be separated? Mr Chan is proceeding for completion of the sale contract against Ocean Distribution. That has no bearing on my client, who was a mere negotiator. The second issue touches him, however: the fraud and conspiracy.'

'On that we agree, Mr Ward. So . . . ?'

'So my understanding is that we should not be talking about the two sets of documentation that you have before you, Master. Rather, we should be investigating the existence of a *third* set of papers.'

'What set?' Simes David rumbled.

'The missing set, which outline a separate agreement—namely, three one-year charters, in place of the ones placed before you.'

'What is this?' Simes David muttered angrily.

Charles Davison rose quickly to his feet. 'This issue is not one we wish to be raised at this stage, Master. It is a contention for trial—and it is basic to our case for fraud and conspiracy. We do not bring it to your attention.'

Simes David glowered. 'But Mr Ward does.'

'I contend—'

'Don't *be* contentious, Mr Davison. Mr Ward is entitled to his opening statement, as you were.'

Charles Davison sank back in his seat. He was not happy with the rebuke. Simon Chan did not look at him. He was staring at Eric, as he continued.

'My client's contention is that he has been drawn into a dispute between the plaintiff and the first defendant against a background of circumstances over which he had no control. The facts he puts before you are these. Mr Reynolds negotiated a contract of sale and charter back of the *Arctic Queen* between the two named parties. He left the meeting to arrange a draft of that agreement. It was that agreement which was signed by both parties.'

'You're talking about the three-year charter?'

'That is so.' Eric paused. 'In the meanwhile, outside

the process of that negotiation, further agreements were reached by the plaintiff and first defendant. Mr Staughton and Mr Lintern negotiated a different arrangement. It was to execute three one-year charters.'

'To what end?' Simes David asked in surprise. 'It would mean the same thing.'

'The reason given was that this would assist Malaysia Mobile in matters of taxation in Kuala Lumpur.'

Charles Davison bobbed up again. 'There is no such relevant restriction in Malaysia. We put no such agreements into evidence. And these issues relate to trial, not this hearing—'

'Mr Davison . . .' Simes David leaned back easily in his chair, a cold light in his pale eyes. 'I am a searcher after truth. When you are older in years, wisdom and discretion, who knows? It may be that you will be elevated to a similar position. But this is *my* hearing. I am also a confused man. I would like to seek clarification. Your interruptions tend to prevent that. So, I would appreciate a degree of prudence, and a greater degree of . . . control.'

There was a menace in the words, which hung in the air after the words themselves had faded in the silence. Simes David glared at Eric. 'These three charter agreements: they are not included in your supporting documentation.'

'I would think you have the first of them in Malaysia Mobile's submission, Master.'

'Huh . . . And the others?'

'My client has no knowledge of them.'

'And this . . . negotiation between Mr Lintern and Mr Staughton: do you have documentation?'

'My client was not a party to that negotiation.'

Simes David grunted in annoyance and glared around the room. 'We're running around in circles here. Have I got the full case before me, or not?'

'The trial—' Davison began.

'I'm not talking about *trial*,' Simes David snapped. 'I'm talking about insufficient documentation at this hearing.

Mr Ward is saying his client has been dragged into a business that was none of his affair. And neither plaintiff nor defendant has filed papers that show an involvement by Mr Reynolds. Now is there further documentation, or not? And if there is—where is it?'

Simon Chan leaned towards Charles Davison and began to whisper in his ear. Paul Lintern watched them for a few moments, then glared at Eric. He was clearly beginning to regret his conversation at the Reform Club. Simes David waited for a few moments, but his patience was wearing thin. 'All right. Mr Davison, do you wish to enter any further documents?'

Charles Davison started. 'Master, these are not issues we want dealt with in a preliminary hearing. We are in no position—'

'Mr Patrick?' Simes David interrupted dismissively.

The Ocean Distribution lawyer cleared his throat. 'We wish to put in no supplementary documentation at this time, Master.'

Simes David heaved a sigh. 'All right. So let me sum up. Malaysia Mobile and Ocean Distribution have one thing in common: they want a decision on merits, on the issues they've raised, and none other. But that seems to me to put a problem on my desk: these issues do not involve Mr Reynolds. This, I believe, is Mr Ward's contention. Mr Ward—you tell me you place no further documentation before me?'

'We have none, Master. And I see no clear reason why International Charters and Mr Reynolds are parties to this action.'

Simes David shook his heavy head, growling low in his throat. He glared at each of the lawyers in turn, and scowled. 'I can get very bad-tempered when I'm being led up a garden path. I'm going to take an adjournment, gentlemen, and a cup of coffee. I suggest you confer among yourselves, because if I don't get some clear answers after the adjournment, I'm going to dismiss Mr Reynolds and International Charters from this case. Do I make myself clear?'

'Master, you can't—' Charles Davison began.

Simes David silenced him with a look. Davison reddened, and sat back in his chair. A heavy silence lay on the room. Simes David turned to Davison's client and rose to his feet. 'Mr Chan, a word of advice. Tell Mr Davison he's not acting in your best interests, with these comments on my power and authority!'

As he swept from the room, Simon Chan sat impassively, staring straight ahead of him, with his hands linked together in his lap.

2

Les Reynolds bubbled with enthusiasm, scratching his thatch of hair enthusiastically. 'That was great, Mr Ward! It seems to be going really well. Do you think he's going to throw out my name from the suit?'

'Don't get too carried away,' Eric warned. 'Those were opening shots. Once Davison and Patrick have had a chance to confer, I think they'll both change their tacks. Not because of your position, but because of their own. The Master is putting pressure on over the other documentation.'

Reynolds licked his lips. 'This other documentation you're talking about. I don't know about it.'

Eric looked at him coolly. 'Neither do I. I'm just making an assumption. You told me Lintern and Staughton reached an agreement when you weren't present.'

'So it seems.' Reynolds agreed. 'The variation on the charter arrangements.'

'Well, one can assume it was reduced to writing in some form. Where is it? That's all I am asking for. And the other two one-year charters: where are they?'

'Nothing to do with me, Mr Ward.'

Eric gave him a level stare. 'So you tell me. And so I've told Simes David,' he added warningly.

Reynolds looked across the room to where the others stood in two tightly-knit groups. 'Will they be consulting with you?'

'I doubt it,' Eric replied grimly. 'They're discussing battle tactics, but now the guns could swing our way. They neither of them are happy about the way things are going, so Davison is likely to come clean on the fraud issue and Patrick will attack on the three-charter problem.'

'Where does that leave me?' Reynolds asked almost plaintively.

'As Simes David put it—piggy in the middle.'

When they had reconvened in the Master's chambers, Simes David placed the palms of his hands on the table in front of him and rumbled, 'Do I detect signs of some kind of decision-making among those present?'

Charles Davison stood up. 'Master—'

Simes David turned to Eric. 'I will allow Mr Davison to speak, assuming you have no objection. You hadn't finished your statement, I think.'

'I'm happy to stand down for the moment, Master, provided I have the right to speak further, if necessary.'

Simes David nodded. 'Proceed, Mr Davison.'

Charles Davison's handsome face was slightly flushed. There was an edge of irritation in his voice. Eric suspected he had been lectured by Simon Chan as well as Simes David, and he was being forced to a course of action he did not want to follow. 'Master, I refer to the issues raised in relation to conspiracy.'

'Good.'

'With reluctance.'

Simes David glowered, but made no comment.

'My client's contention is simply stated,' Davison went on. 'We put into the hearing no series of other documentation, for in our contention the original agreement—the single one-year charter—is all that is necessary. It is a binding agreement entered into by Mr Staughton and Mr Lintern for their respective companies.'

'So?'

'That document supports our claim for the purchase price to be paid, with costs. As for the conspiracy and fraud issues, they are a separate matter. We would wish to pursue the argument already touched upon by Mr Ward—namely, the agreement between Mr Lintern and Mr Staughton which was outside the terms of the document in our possession. That agreement, we argue, was entered into with the knowledge and connivance of Mr Reynolds, and that is the reason why he is made a party to the claim in fraud and conspiracy.'

The room fell silent as Davison sat down. Simes David looked at Eric, but Eric made no response. Les Reynolds was still, the tension in his body communicated to Eric. Simes David sighed.

'Mr Davison, that's fine, it clears the decks somewhat . . . but there's nothing filed to support your argument.'

'It was not our intention to so argue today, Master. Our hand has been forced.'

'All right,' Simes David said, shrugging. 'Let's hear from you, Mr Patrick.'

The thin-faced lawyer stood up. 'My client will, of course, resist the claim in fraud and conspiracy. Our contention is quite clear. The condition precedent for the sale was a three-year charter. At the instigation of the Charter Manager for Malaysia Mobile, Mr Lintern, and the board of Ocean Distribution, was persuaded to agree to three one-year charters. The first of these has been filed. The others have yet to be completed. The minutes of the relevant board meeting of Ocean Distribution are now tendered in support of this statement.'

Simes David was not pleased. He would clearly have preferred to receive the papers at an earlier date. He pushed them aside dismissively. 'Board minutes are one thing: a documented agreement is another. Reference has been made to other papers, concerning this three-year charter arrangement. Board minutes are hardly persuasive: where is the actual agreement?'

Paul Lintern wriggled uncomfortably in his chair. Eric stared at him, suddenly wondering. He watched, as Lintern began to whisper urgently to his lawyer.

Eric turned to Les Reynolds in the pause. 'Davison is claiming you were party to the Lintern–Staughton discussions. Were you?'

'I told you, Mr Ward. I wasn't there.'

Eric frowned. 'Did you have no inkling of the further arrangements made between Lintern and Staughton?' he whispered.

'I swear to you,' Reynolds replied hoarsely, 'I went out to draft the original agreement for the three-year charter. They came to their private arrangement after that.'

'And Staughton said nothing to you?'

'No.'

'So Staughton conned you as well as Lintern and Chan.'

'That's exactly the way of it,' Reynolds insisted.

Evan Patrick was about to speak.

'The position is, Master, that the agreement reached between Mr Lintern and Mr Staughton is not available. My client is prepared to testify on oath that such an agreement was made and can produce the evidence of a three-year charter, signed by Mr Staughton. The agreement behind that, relating to three one-year charters, was retained by Mr Staughton, and is not available to Ocean Distribution.'

'*You can't be serious!*' Simes David exploded. 'A copy wasn't kept by Mr Lintern?'

Evan Patrick's voice wavered. 'No, Master.'

'Are these experienced *businessmen* we're dealing with?' Simes David asked sarcastically. 'Are we really saying that normal business practices haven't been followed? Mr Davison, you want to interpose.'

'Yes, Master. If the Lintern–Staughton agreement can't

be placed before you, that's a problem for the defence. But any such agreement is in fact irrelevant—as is the copy of the three-year charter already filed.'

Simes David raised his eyebrows. 'Why so?'

'Mr Staughton had no authority to enter into such charter arrangements, none beyond a one-year agreement. That is specifically stated in his terms of employment.'

'Mr Patrick?'

Evan Patrick consulted the papers in front of him. 'I refer you to the case of the *Royal British Bank v Turquand*, Master. Mr Staughton was Vice President and Charter Manager of Malaysia Mobile. In such a position he was held out by his employers to have all the powers a Charter Manager would normally have. As far as my clients are concerned, that would include the authority to enter into any charter arrangements. *Turquand's Case* emphasizes that it is not the duty of my clients to seek out the internal arrangements made between Mr Staughton and Malaysia Mobile: it is sufficient that he was held out as having that authority.' Evan Patrick flashed a glance in Davison's direction. 'Consequently, the three-year charter *is* relevant—it is a complete answer to the claim brought by the plaintiffs.'

Simes David heaved a sigh of despondency. 'I keep hearing about this Mr Staughton. He appears to me to be central to the whole issue. But he has not been named as a party, and he makes no appearance. Can anyone explain why this is so?'

There was a short silence. Charles Davison rose to his feet, reluctantly. 'Mr Staughton is dead, Master. He was murdered, in Spain.'

The Master stared disbelievingly at Davison and the silence grew heavily around them. Simes David sniffed and looked around the room. 'Murdered . . .' He shook his head. 'All right. So where do we go from here? I am clearly being asked to make a ruling on whether there is a case to answer in view of Mr Staughton's ostensible authority or lack of it. I am being asked to agree a defence which relies upon non-existent documents. I am presented with two conflicting charters—one for three years and one for one year—both signed by Mr Lintern and the deceased Mr Staughton. The dates on each are the same. I am aware of no precedent which suggests to me that the one should supersede the other. On the other hand, the fact of an agreement relating to three years is supported by the board minutes, it is claimed, from Ocean Distribution. When I've had time to read them, I'll be able to confirm, or disagree with, that point of view. But I am forced to say I am extremely unhappy.'

Evan Patrick shuffled in his chair, and Davison glanced at Eric, frowning.

'I am left with the impression,' Simes David continued, 'that everything that could be said is not being said in this case. An effort to simplify matters has been made by the plaintiffs—but they have succeeded in over-simplification. Ocean Distribution rely upon a signed, three-year charter as a defence, but cannot satisfactorily explain the one-year charter arrangement which also bears Mr Lintern's signature. There is no documentation, other than the charter, to support it. And nowhere does the second defendant, Mr Reynolds, appear, as they say in racing circles, in the frame . . .' He paused and looked at Eric. 'Mr Ward, are you now prepared to make a submission for Mr Reynolds to be struck out of this case?'

Eric rose and nodded. 'Yes, Master, I formally request that—'

'*But dammit, he was there when we made the agreement!*'

The words had burst, almost involuntarily, from Paul Lintern. White-faced and furious at the thought that he was being left alone in the firing line, he glared at Les Reynolds. 'You're not walking away from this! You were there! You know Staughton set up a second agreement!'

Eric stood still. He looked down at his client. Reynolds was ashen-faced, his earlier enthusiasm evaporated. He caught Eric's glance and shook his head. 'I swear, Mr Ward . . .'

Eric didn't believe him.

Simes David was pointing a hairy finger at Paul Lintern. 'Mr Lintern, this is not a court of law, and I prefaced my remarks by saying we would not be indulging in formal legal procedures. Nevertheless, you have lawyers to represent you. On the whole, they know how to conduct themselves. You clearly do not. If I get another outburst like that, I'll have you out of my chambers!' He paused, threateningly, then turned his heavy head in Eric's direction. 'You were saying, Mr Ward . . .'

'I . . . I was requesting that my client be dismissed from this case, Master.'

'And Mr Lintern's *ex cathedra* comments?' Simes David asked sarcastically, glancing at Lintern's angry features.

Eric hesitated. 'My instructions are clear, Master. It's up to Mr Lintern to produce evidence—'

'Hmmm.' Simes David was scowling, his dark eyebrows drawn together. 'More and more I get the impression I'm not being told everything. On the other hand, nothing has been presented to me to suggest that Mr Reynolds is in any way involved in what seems to me to be a straightforward disagreement between Malaysia Mobile and Ocean Distribution. There is certainly no evidence laid before me to suggest fraud and conspiracy—'

'That is for trial, Master!' Davison interposed hotly.

'—so I am prepared to accept your submission, Mr Ward. And as for you, Mr Davison, one more outburst of this kind from you, and Mr Chan will have to seek another lawyer.'

Eric began to gather up his papers. He felt no pleasure in his achievement; it was as though there was a heavy weight in his stomach. Les Reynolds looked up at him, his eyes nervous and evasive. 'Does that mean it's over, Mr Ward?'

'It does,' Eric replied, staring down at him. He was now

certain Reynolds had lied. He had known about the second agreement; he might well have been present during the discussions. But he would never admit to it, and the relevant documentation was missing. It would be Lintern's word against his, since the third party, Harry Staughton, was dead. Reynolds was leaving Lintern exposed to face the music. The devil take the hindmost, Eric thought cynically. He gathered up his papers, but his mind was spinning; he paused, and he looked at Lintern, his face twisted with anger and frustration, and at Simon Chan, placid, unmoved by the bitterness around him. He thought of Greg Bowles, sneering in Singapore at the way he had put one over on the man who was to steal his wife. A knot of anger gathered in Eric's chest; everything had not been said, and perhaps it was time the questions were put.

'Master, may I make some further comments?' Eric said suddenly.

Simes David glowered at him. 'I would have thought you'd have been only too pleased to turn your back on this mess, Mr Ward. You are—'

'Master! I must protest,' Charles Davison exploded. 'Mr Ward no longer has status in this hearing.'

Simes David smiled thinly, wickedly; he looked upon Davison with a beam that was almost benevolent, as he said, 'I was *about* to comment to Mr Ward that he was now no longer at issue in this hearing, with the dismissal of his client from the suit, so he has no status. I was *about* to say I would not hear him. However, I am now changing my mind. This is my hearing, Mr Davison; these are my chambers. And I'll hear anyone I like!' He turned to Eric. 'Please, Mr Ward,' he said sweetly, 'if you have anything to say which might expedite or clarify these proceedings, I'd be delighted to listen to you . . .'

3

Eric stood there for several seconds, his mind churning over the events of the last few weeks, the information he had gleaned from Chan and Lintern, Bowles and Reynolds, and O'Connor, and he began to see a pattern, a rationale behind the confusion of events. It had to be tested, of course, but Simes David was giving him the chance to test it before an objective audience.

'Master, if I may crave your indulgence for a few minutes, it's possible I could bring some clarification into these proceedings.'

'Anything, Mr Ward,' Simes David groaned theatrically.

'It will be necessary for me to hypothecate,' Eric warned.

'The law is full of deemings and hypothecations,' Simes David replied, almost cheerfully. 'It's one of its more attractive features, don't you agree, gentlemen?'

The faces of his audience suggested otherwise: Simon Chan was looking wary beside the open-mouthed, annoyed Davison; Lintern's features expressed open fear, while Patrick was nonplussed. Les Reynolds sat stiffly beside Eric, his hands gripping the table edge in front of him. It all cheered Simes David up even further. 'Please, Mr Ward—hypothecate.'

'You yourself have remarked, Master, that all that could be said doesn't seem to be emerging. I agree. I also draw attention to and emphasize something else you touched upon. Namely, the curious fact that experienced businessmen seem to have behaved in an unbusinesslike fashion.'

'Precisely,' Simes David agreed happily.

'Not only have they not taken basic business precautions, but they also appear to have been—for experienced businessmen—remarkably gullible. We have not had the privilege of hearing or seeing Mr Staughton, but we have been led to believe, first, that my own client, Mr Reynolds, was misled and, indeed cheated by Mr Staughton. Second, we have the experienced firm of Ocean Distribution entering an agreement through their managing director, Mr Lintern, who also was gulled by Mr Staughton. Persuaded in fact, to vary an agreement—in front of, or away from Mr Reynolds—which is now the subject of this suit. Thirdly, we have the employers themselves, and Mr Simon Chan, equally fooled by their own Vice President and Charter Manager.'

'What a falling off is here!' Simes David said, smiling.

'I find it extremely difficult to believe that three such experienced businessmen could have been conned and misled so comprehensively by the deceased Mr Staughton,' Eric continued. 'So, pursuing that thought, perhaps we should look at other possibilities.'

'Such as?'

'The thought that they were *not* misled at all.'

Simes David leaned back in his chair and slowly looked around the room, his glance resting on each of the participants in turn: Simon Chan, Paul Lintern and Les Reynolds. 'The level of my interest is rising, Mr Ward.'

'At this point I must extend my hypothesis,' Eric explained. He paused: the cold weight in his stomach was still there, and the wound in his arm was beginning to throb, a reminder of a struggle in the dark. 'If we allow the possibility I've suggested, perhaps I could sketch a hypothetical scenario to explain it. First of all, there's the *Arctic Queen* herself. She was barely seaworthy—yet Staughton arranged her purchase, through Reynolds, from a man called Bowles, who was pleased to make what he thought was a financial killing. Why would Staughton do that? Possibly because he saw the opportunity to make money for himself.'

'And how could he do that, Mr Ward?'

'By entering into a spurious contract with others. By selling the vessel on to another party, who was prepared to talk about kickbacks.'

Simes David frowned thoughtfully. 'I think you're beginning to make large assumptions.'

ashen, and Les Reynolds squirmed awkwardly beside him. But it was Simon Chan whom Eric observed most keenly: the impassive Chinese businessman showed no emotion, but perhaps that in itself was a sign of his tension: he was controlling his feelings and his external appearance with an iron will.

'I was first called into this matter,' Eric said, 'by Mr Chan, who told me Harry Staughton had stolen money from his company. In effect, it was the first tranche of the purchase price of the *Arctic Queen*. Then Mr Reynolds asked me to defend him against the charge of fraud and conspiracy—which has not really been properly laid today. But why is that? Because Mr Chan can't prove it without showing the missing documentation. And he might not want to do that.'

'To prove his case with the documentation?' Simes David asked. 'Why on earth not?'

'Because of its provenance. *He could have got it only from Staughton.*'

Eric glanced at Paul Lintern. 'A similar situation bedevils Mr Lintern. He could prove the existence of a binding agreement with Staughton over the three one-year charters—but if he has a copy, as I imagine he does, he can't produce it because it would show he has defrauded his own board. There was the chance the other copy could come to light, of course—Staughton's copy.'

Eric paused. 'And then we have Mr Reynolds. He's told me consistently he wasn't involved in the second agreement. Mr Lintern says otherwise. Was Mr Reynolds a party? Does he also have a copy? That documentation could show that he too has a case to answer—fraud against Malaysia Mobile. So he dare not disclose it—if he's involved.'

Simes David was watching Eric narrowly, weighing up arguments that were nothing to do with the issues in the civil suit. He waited, and the atmosphere in the chambers was electric.

'So all this emphasizes that the papers held by Harry

Staughton were important. Chan wanted them, to prove fraud. To Reynolds and Lintern they were dangerous—they could undermine their defence against fraud. And all three had a grudge against Staughton—he'd cost each of them a lot of money. The question is: which of them felt so strongly about it that he took steps to get Staughton killed and the papers retrieved, or maybe destroyed?'

Charles Davison cleared his throat. He stood up and began to gather his papers, as though to stress that, with the hearing over, none of them had to listen further to Eric. After a few moments, when no one else moved, he sat down again.

'You have a view, I imagine,' Simes David said thoughtfully, 'within your hypothesis.'

'I have a fact, also, Master. I believe the actual killer of Harry Staughton—and, incidentally, Greg Bowles's wife—is presently in custody.'

Heads turned quickly. Someone let out a long hiss of surprise. Simon Chan did not move. Eric looked at him, and smiled thinly.

'*You* won't be surprised, of course, Mr Chan. Your network of informers will already have told you that Soldier Mason has been arrested—if only for credit card fraud.'

Chan looked at him, his head turning slowly. He said nothing.

'So, apart from Greg Bowles, who hated Staughton for stealing his wife, there were three people who could want Staughton dead and the papers destroyed. I think all three of them have been looking for Staughton. But only one of them succeeded in finding him, perhaps because he knew him well.' Eric paused, looking across the room to the Chinese businessman. 'Chan knew Staughton was dead, shortly after it happened. He told me. Lintern *might* have known but I've no way of checking on that. But when I told Les Reynolds that Staughton was dead, he was clearly taken by surprise—shaken by the information.'

'So are you suggesting that *I* could have been responsible

for Staughton's murder?' Paul Lintern flared. 'That's crazy! He'd conned me, defrauded me, left me to face problems with my board, but there was no way I would have sorted it out by killing him!'

Simes David raised a hand, silencing him, his eyes still fixed on Eric. 'Go on, Mr Ward.'

'It wasn't just Staughton who had to be killed,' Eric replied. 'There was Leah Bowles, too. She could identify the killer; and the killer could identify the man who'd hired him. So Leah had to be removed. The trouble was, she'd escaped the first murderous attack and was hiding in England. But she did contact someone in England, refusing to meet him, but asking for the name of a lawyer she could trust. My name was given to her. And when I went to see her, I was followed. The man who followed me, killed her—and, incidentally, took a slice out of my arm.'

Charles Davison muttered something to Simon Chan. Eric could guess it would not be complimentary to him.

'So the central question is, who sent me to Leah Bowles? For that will be the same person who sent the killer to Harry Staughton.' Eric paused. 'Chan, who had already used me? Lintern, who knew I was looking for Staughton?' Eric grimaced. 'I said a few moments ago that one man was surprised, when I told him that Staughton was dead. I made an assumption from that: I assumed from his obvious surprise that he didn't know Staughton had been murdered. But when I thought back over the words used, I realized I was wrong.'

Beside Eric, Les Reynolds stirred.

'The words you used, Mr Reynolds, were *How did you know that?*'

'I don't see—'

'When you came to my office you were genuinely surprised, right enough—but not that Staughton was dead. You were surprised because I *knew* about it!'

'I can't—'

'You were in the north. Leah Bowles phoned you, as an

old friend. You tried to get her to disclose her address. When she wouldn't, but asked you for the name of a lawyer, you gave her my name and instructed the killer to follow me. And you then had the nerve to come to me, to ask me to represent you in this action today. But seconds after you left me, she phoned, and you discovered I already knew Staughton was dead! It put your plan in jeopardy. I might have gone to the police. But I didn't. I went ahead . . . and led your hired killer to Leah Bowles.'

Les Reynolds made no reply. Simes David stared at him for several seconds. Then, heavily, before he rose to his feet, the Master said, 'That's enough.' He gazed cynically in Reynolds's direction. 'If I were you, Mr Reynolds, I'd get myself a lawyer. That is,' he added, glancing at Eric, '*another* lawyer. I don't imagine Mr Ward would take your brief.'

4

Anne brought the long, legal envelope to Eric as he sat sprawled on the terrace at Sedleigh Hall, enjoying the sunshine and flexing his wounded arm. She sat down beside him, perching on the low wall and squinting up into the sun. 'You just missed the news on the radio.'

'Anything interesting?'

'The Iberica bid has collapsed. Your department of dirty tricks has worked well.'

'Phil Cooper's articles, you mean.'

'You fed him the stuff. I imagine Leonard Channing will soon be on the phone to congratulate you.'

'That'll be the day! You must be joking. Leonard will take the credit, at the board, that's all. But don't imagine I'm too happy about the campaign—it's not something I'd like to get involved with again.'

'What was the phone call about, while I was upstairs?'

Eric looked at her solemnly. 'I trust you weren't listening on the extension. I mean, how can my fancy woman get in touch if you're listening like that?'

'It wasn't a woman. It was a man's voice.'

'Tony O'Connor. He rang to tell me that Soldier Mason wants to do a deal. Forensic have managed to find some hairs which match up to Leah Bowles's killing, so he's decided to do the Queen's Evidence bit, try to get some leniency for coming clean about Les Reynolds.'

'Will they agree that?' Anne asked, scandalized.

Eric shrugged. 'They may soft pedal a bit, unofficially, because the case against Les Reynolds was always going to be difficult to prove without Mason's cooperation.' He slit open the envelope. 'And this seems to be the judgement of Master Simes David . . .'

He read it quickly, and smiled. 'Succinct and direct.'

'What's he saying?'

'Effectively, a plague on both their houses. I quote:

' "It is clear from internal evidence that Mr Staughton had no authority to enter the three-year charter agreement. It is argued that he had ostensible authority so to do. But Mr Lintern knew the authority was lacking. Consequently, there could be no binding agreement regarding that charter.

' "Evidence for the one-year charter agreement is lacking: it has not been produced. No contract can therefore be based on that issue, other than the document produced by Mr Lintern. Standing against another, conflicting document with his signature, it can give rise to no binding agreement.

' "Since the charters were not binding, and since a charter agreement was a condition precedent on the sale of the vessel, there could be no binding sale agreement. It follows that if there was no sale agreement, ownership of the *Arctic Queen* must revert to Malaysia Mobile. As to the loss sustained, it must lie where it falls." '

Eric began to laugh.

'What's it all mean?' Anne asked.

'It means Simon Chan's stuck with a worthless vessel; Ocean Distribution have lost a lot of money; Paul Lintern will get thrown out; and if they ever find the money that

Staughton stashed away somewhere the lawyers will have a field day claiming just who it belongs to.'

'Harry Staughton left quite a legacy.'

'That's right. He came like a thief in the night to steal Greg Bowles's wife, Simon Chan's money, Les Reynolds's commission and Paul Lintern's secret profit. It was all the kind of transaction that gives business a bad name. He paid for it, of course.'

'With his life.'

'And Leah's.'

'I wonder if he loved her,' Anne asked, half to herself.

Eric wondered, too. But he had never got close to the real Harry Staughton, in all the time he'd spent thinking about him.

'I guess we'll never know,' he said.